The Ghost's Grave

The Ghost's Grave

The
Ghost's

Grave

PEG KEHRET

SCHOLASTIC INC.

New York Toronto London Auckland Sydney
Mexico City New Delhi Hong Kong Buenos Aires

No part of this publication may be reproduced, stored in a retrieval system, or transmitted in any form or by any means, electronic, mechanical, photocopying, recording, or otherwise, without written permission of the publisher. For information regarding permission, write to Dutton Children's Books, a member of Penguin Group (USA) Inc., 375 Hudson Street, New York, NY 10014.

ISBN-13: 978-0-439-89976-5
ISBN-10: 0-439-89976-1

12 11 10 9 8 7 6 5 4 3   6 7 8 9 10 11/0

Printed in the U.S.A.   40

First Scholastic printing, October 2006

Designed by Gloria Cheng

*For Carl, who built the world's best
tree house in my woods,
and for Eric, Mark, Chelsea, and Brett,
who fill it with fun*

ACKNOWLEDGMENTS

This is the seventeenth book that Rosanne Lauer has edited for me. She always suggests ways that I can improve my original manuscript. I value her skills and cherish her friendship.

I thank Andrea Mosbacher for her careful copyediting. She saves me from embarrassing myself when she corrects my spelling and punctuation.

Lori Robinson and Pam Knight of the Enumclaw, Washington, branch of Bank of America answered my questions about counterfeit money and showed me stacks of one-hundred-dollar bills so that I could correctly describe their size.

Frank Hall helped me write accurately about emergency medical technicians. *Mining Tragedies in Carbon River Coal Country*, transcribed and edited by Stephen K. Meitzler, was a useful publication.

Special thanks to everyone at Dutton Children's Books for their support over the many years I've been a Dutton author.

The Ghost's Grave

CHAPTER ONE

The night I moved in with Aunt Ethel, she shot a bat in the kitchen. If there had been anyplace else for me to go, I would have headed back to the airport right then. Of course, if I'd had a choice of where to spend the summer, I would never have trudged into Aunt Ethel's house in the first place.

After a plane ride from Minneapolis to Seattle; a shuttle ride downtown to the Greyhound bus station; and a long, bumpy bus ride to Carbon City, I saw Aunt Ethel for the first time.

She met me at the bus station. It wasn't really a station—there was merely a sign in the window of the Carbon City Market: BUS ARRIVES AND DEPARTS HERE. ASK FOR SCHEDULE.

While the bus driver unloaded my bag and my

box of books from the luggage area beneath the bus, I glanced around. Carbon City wasn't much of a city. The Market was a small general store, flanked by an empty building that had the words CARBON CITY HOTEL, 1911 embedded in its bricks, and by a post office the size of a bathroom.

A scattering of houses backed up to the hills on either side of the road. In one yard a faded FOR SALE BY OWNER sign looked as if it had been there long enough to grow roots. Next door, tall grass had grown up through the spokes of a discarded bicycle, and a black cat dozed on the hood of a car that had no tires. Dusk darkened the street, making it seem dreary, but I suspected Carbon City would be bleak in full sun, too. The town matched my mood.

"You can put your gear in the back," Aunt Ethel said, pointing across the street to an old red pickup truck. Rust spots dotted the truck's dented sides, and strips of duct tape held the rear window together.

The truck had seen better days, and so had Aunt Ethel. Her face was as lined as a road map. She wore a shapeless pink cotton dress, a brown cardigan sweater with holes in the elbows, and sturdy laced shoes. White hair, which looked as if she trimmed it herself, formed an irregular cloud around her head.

Mom had warned me not to be guilty of ageism.

"Being elderly doesn't mean she won't be interesting."

"She's seventy years older than I am," I had said. "What will we talk about?"

"Ask about her childhood. Ask her about the history of Carbon City; it's an old coal-mining town."

As I climbed into the truck, I thought the complete history of Carbon City would probably take at least two minutes. I noticed the bus driver quickly turned around and headed back the way we'd come.

I put my backpack on the floor, then felt over my shoulder and on the seat for my seat belt.

"Did you drop something?" Aunt Ethel asked as she turned the key. The truck made a grinding sound.

"I'm looking for my seat belt."

"Don't have any. I bought my truck long before seat belts were invented."

Hoo boy, I thought. Mom will have a fit about this.

Aunt Ethel turned the key off, pumped the gas pedal a few times, then turned the key on again. The grinding sound returned.

"Fleas and mosquitoes!" Aunt Ethel cried. "This is no time to be temperamental." She whacked the dashboard with her fist.

The grinding sound quit as the truck roared to life, belching a cloud of black smoke into the street.

Apparently, the truck was built before emissions standards, too.

I didn't try to make conversation on the drive home; I was too scared to talk. Riding with Aunt Ethel made the thrill rides at the state fair seem tame. Her truck straddled the center line of the road, even when we went around curves. The engine backfired regularly, a loud *Bang! Pop!* noise. Each time it happened, the truck jerked forward erratically. Wondering whether Aunt Ethel had ever bothered to get a driver's license, I clenched my teeth and braced myself for the crash.

Luckily, we met no oncoming cars, a clue that nobody else went where I was headed. We banged and popped our way out of Carbon City, up a wooded hill, and past an old cemetery. We curved first left and then right and finally turned down a long gravel road.

When my nerves were totally frazzled, we lurched to a stop in front of an old two-story wooden house. By then the darkness was complete, with no street lamps or neighboring lights to serve as beacons. The run-down house loomed in the headlights, the perfect setting for a horror movie.

"Here we are," Aunt Ethel said.

The truck gave a final hiccup as I lifted my suitcase out. I followed Aunt Ethel into the house.

The second she turned on the light, Aunt Ethel screamed. Let me tell you, that woman's voice is louder than a fire engine's siren.

I jumped, then dropped my suitcase with a thud.

"Open the doors!" she yelled. "Hurry!"

"What's wrong?" I reached behind me to open the door we'd just closed.

"There's a bat in here. Get it out! Out!"

I followed her gaze upward and saw a bat circling the ceiling fan.

While I ran from room to room, looking for outside doors to open, she grabbed a broom and chased the bat.

Mom had once told me, "Bats get a bad rap. People should encourage bats to stay, not chase them off."

Aunt Ethel did not encourage her bat to stay.

Whoosh! Whoosh! She swung the broom at the bat as it zigzagged above us.

Aunt Ethel's house has high ceilings, so her broom couldn't reach the bat, but she looped it overhead in figure eights anyway.

I opened the kitchen door and flipped a light switch, illuminating a patch of grass and a flower bed. "Maybe if we leave him alone, he'll fly out by himself," I said.

"And maybe he won't."

I couldn't argue with her logic.

"Mom says bats are good," I told her. "They eat mosquitoes."

"Well, this one should have eaten his mosquitoes outside," Aunt Ethel said. "I don't want any bat landing in *my* hair."

It seemed unlikely the bat would want to land in her hair, with her head bobbing up and down and twisting back and forth like a roller coaster as she watched him.

The bat flew around the living room; Aunt Ethel leaped on the sofa and waved the broom at him.

I knew that some people have irrational fears of harmless creatures. Mom freaks out when she sees a spider, and my best friend back in Vermont was scared of garter snakes. Apparently Aunt Ethel feared bats.

The bat swooped into the kitchen.

"That does it!" Aunt Ethel hollered. "I will not allow bat droppings in my kitchen."

She flung the broom to the floor, ran upstairs to her bedroom, and returned with a shotgun.

I followed her to the kitchen, trying to talk sense into her. "If we turn off the lights in here and leave the porch lights on, he'll probably fly out one of the doors."

She raised the gun, then swayed from side to side as she tried to keep the bat in the site.

"Aunt Ethel! No! You'll blow a hole in the house."

BAM!!

I may never hear well again. The shot reverberated through the kitchen, out the front door, and probably all the way back to Minneapolis where, three short weeks earlier, I had been an average twelve-and-a-half-year-old boy, dreaming of playing on a summer baseball team and leading a normal life. Now I'd moved in with a lunatic.

When my ears quit ringing, I opened my eyes, which was the first I realized I had squeezed them shut. I didn't have to ask if Aunt Ethel had hit her mark. Blood spattered the front of the kitchen cabinets. The refrigerator looked as if it had the measles. Red dots covered the floor like confetti. How could one little bat contain so much fluid?

I didn't see a hole in the wall. I didn't see a dead bat, either. Had she only wounded him? Was he now flapping about in the living room, dripping blood on the furniture?

"Did you kill him?" I asked.

"Of course I killed him. Your auntie's a crack shot." She closed the kitchen door that led outside, removed her sweater, and poured herself a drink of water.

"Where is he?"

She pointed. "He fell on top of the cupboard. I'll have to get the ladder."

While I dampened a paper towel and used it to mop bat blood from the stove burners, Aunt Ethel left with the gun and returned with a rickety yellow ladder. She took a plastic bag from a drawer—I assumed it would be a bat "body bag." She climbed up the ladder until she could see the top of the cupboard.

"Hmm," she said. She stepped to the countertop and peered at the back of the cupboard.

"Is it there?" I asked.

"The bat fell down behind the cupboard," she said.

"What? How could it?"

"The cupboard doesn't hang straight. It's tight at the bottom but not at the top, so there's space between the back of the cupboard and the wall. The bat fell down in that space, and it's lodged back there."

I eyeballed the cupboard from the side; she was right. The cupboard top stuck out from the wall about an inch. There wasn't room to reach down behind it. "How are we going to get the bat out of there?"

"We aren't."

I gaped at the white-haired woman who stood on the kitchen counter. Her pink cotton dress was so wrinkled, I wondered if it doubled as her nightgown.

"You're going to leave a dead bat behind the cupboard?"

"There's no way to fish it out, short of tearing the cupboard off the wall. The bat's dead, that's for sure, so we'll let it rest in peace behind the cupboard."

"Won't it smell?"

"If it starts to smell, I'll deal with it then," she said. She climbed down, put the ladder away, and started washing the refrigerator.

"Shouldn't we close the front door?" I said. "We wouldn't want another bat to come in."

"I shut the door when I went after the ladder."

I finished cleaning the stove and started wiping spots from the floor. I wanted to say, *Wouldn't it have been simpler to wait for the bat to leave?* Instead, I worked in silence.

The truth is, I felt sorry for the bat. It hadn't hurt us. It made one little mistake—flew down the chimney or something—and because of that one small error, it got blown to smithereens and left to rot behind the kitchen cupboard.

I remembered a bat book, *Stellaluna*, that my second-grade teacher had read to the class, and I thought about Mom telling me bats are good. The more I replayed the incident, the more unhappy I felt. Through no fault of its own, the bat was in the wrong place.

Like me, I thought. Through no fault of my own, I was stuck with Aunt Ethel for the next two months. It was a stretch to even call her a relative. She's the great-aunt of my new stepfather, Steven, which makes her my Great-Great-Aunt Ethel, but that's too much of a mouthful. Besides, there wasn't anything great about her that I could see. Nothing great about where she lived, either.

I inquired about the area while we scrubbed the kitchen floor, and what I learned did not brighten my mood. The closest movie theater was eighteen miles away, in the town of Diamond Hill. So was a decent grocery store. As for renting a video, forget it. Even if there had been a video store nearby, which there wasn't, Aunt Ethel doesn't own a VCR or DVD player. She doesn't have a computer, either. No e-mail, no Internet.

"What about television?" I asked. "You *do* have a TV, don't you?" If I couldn't play baseball this summer, at least I could watch it.

"TV's a waste of time. My sister had one, but the programs were junk, so when she passed on, I donated the TV to the Diamond Hill Hospital's thrift shop. Any news I need, I can hear on the radio. Most of it's so depressing, I'm better off not knowing."

No TV. I felt fortunate to have electric lights and indoor plumbing.

The summer stretched before me, one blank calendar square after the next. I understood now why Mom had not objected when I brought my box of books, all my CDs, and my CD player. She and Steven must have known what a desolate place Carbon City is. They had given me glowing reports of the woods and the wildlife but had conveniently forgotten to mention no television and no movies.

"Oh, fleas and mosquitoes," Aunt Ethel said as she picked up a cake plate that held a layer cake with chocolate frosting. "Your welcome cake is ruined." As she dumped it in the garbage container under the sink, I saw that it said WELCOME JOSH in white frosting on top. "Did Steven tell you I'm the Cake Queen of Coal County?"

"No." Steven had failed to tell me a lot of things.

"I bake cakes for special occasions. For years, I delivered them all over the county. Birthday cakes, wedding cakes, baby-shower cakes—you name it, I've baked a cake for it. Once I even made a "Happy Divorce" cake—half white with white frosting and half chocolate with chocolate frosting. The couple split it right down the middle."

She rinsed the cake plate. "My cakes paid off the mortgage on this house—paid for my truck, too. I don't deliver anymore, but my loyal customers still order from me and come to pick the cakes up." She leaned toward me and whispered, "I'll tell you my secret: sour cream."

I blinked at her.

"In the cakes," she explained. "My secret ingredient that makes them so moist and tasty is sour cream."

When we finished cleaning the kitchen, Aunt Ethel showed me around the house. The tour of the downstairs wasn't necessary because I had already run through every room, looking for doors to open. My bedroom was upstairs, next to Aunt Ethel's.

After I put my things in my room, it took me thirty seconds to unpack. I'd brought jeans, shorts, T-shirts, socks, underwear, pajamas, an extra pair of shoes, and two sweatshirts in case it got cool. I left my books in the box.

"Are you hungry?" Aunt Ethel asked from the doorway. "Do you want a snack before you go to bed?"

The bat episode had taken away my appetite. "No, thanks," I said. "I'm fine."

"Good night, then. Help yourself if you get hungry in the night. I'll leave a night-light burning in the bathroom."

After I got in bed, I tried to read for a while, but my brain couldn't concentrate. I turned off the light and lay there listening to the silence.

How am I going to survive this? I wondered. How can I spend the next eight weeks in the middle of nowhere with a crazy woman who drives down the middle of the road and shoots her gun in the kitchen?

CHAPTER TWO

As I stared into the dark, my thoughts drifted back three weeks to the day I found out I'd been selected for the summer baseball team. When I saw my name on the team list, I ran all the way home, eager to share my excitement. Mom might even quit fretting about being unemployed long enough to congratulate me.

I hadn't told Mom and Steven I was trying out because I didn't want to disappoint them if I didn't make it. I knew they were concerned because I had not yet made friends after two months in my new school. Well, they could quit worrying. All my buddies back in Vermont were guys I'd met playing on baseball or basketball teams, and I knew that would happen in Minneapolis, too.

I bounded up the front steps, tossed my backpack

on the hall table, and called, "I'm home!" To my surprise, both Mom and Steven answered. Why was Steven home so early? He never showed up until six-thirty or seven.

They sat at the kitchen table with maps and papers spread out in front of them. Steven, who works as an engineer for a road-building company, often travels for his job; I assumed the maps meant another business trip soon.

"Guess what!" I said. "I tried out for summer baseball, and I made the team!"

Mom looked stunned. "There's a school baseball team during summer vacation?" she asked.

I stood in my batting stance, with an imaginary bat on my shoulder, then swung at the imaginary ball. "It's only for kids going into seventh or eighth grade. Games start the first week of vacation, and we play three times a week through August."

I expected applause. Instead, Mom looked at Steven, the hesitating kind of look that adults give each other when they know something that the kids don't know and are deciding how to tell it.

I was too psyched to wonder what the look meant or to quit talking. "My first practice is tomorrow," I said. "I'll probably play right field."

"Congratulations on making the team," Steven

said, "but . . ." He looked at Mom, as if hoping she would finish the sentence.

"But what?" I sensed something was terribly wrong, though I couldn't imagine what.

"I'm sorry, Josh," Mom said. "You can't be on the team."

"Why not?"

"Steven's being sent to India for two months," Mom said. "You won't be here this summer."

"India!"

I felt as if a vacuum had been switched on somewhere deep inside me, sucking all the happiness out. I slumped onto a chair.

"Making this team is the best thing that's happened to me since I left Vermont," I said. "You want me to participate in school activities; you want me to make friends here. Well, the summer baseball team is my chance to do that."

"I didn't ask for this assignment," Steven said, "and I wish it had come at a different time, but I have to take it. I'm the only engineer in my company who's qualified for this job."

I looked at Mom. "Why do we have to go with him?" I asked. "Why can't we stay here?"

"Steven's boss has hired me as Steven's assistant for the summer," Mom said. "I'll type up all the reports, handle e-mail, and take care of the daily arrangements. It's a temporary job, but it will get my foot in the door and give me a local reference."

"What about me?" I asked. "What am I supposed to do all day while the two of you build roads and type reports?"

"You're going to have a wonderful summer," Mom said.

"In a hotel room in India? Don't count on it."

"You aren't going to India with us," Steven said. "You'll spend the summer in Washington State with my Aunt Ethel."

"Your aunt!" I leaned toward Steven. "I don't even know her."

"You'll like her. She has a big house out in the country—fifty acres, I think. There's a tree house in the woods and wild blackberries to pick. I used to visit her and Aunt Florence every summer when I was a kid."

"I know you're disappointed about the baseball team," Mom said, "and I'm sorry you can't be on it, but you'll have other years to play baseball. This is a once-in-a-lifetime chance for Steven and me."

I looked at the pile of maps, lists, and books about India. "How long have you known about this?" I asked.

"Steven learned about the India assignment last week," Mom said.

"Why didn't you tell me?"

"We wanted to wait until we knew if I'd be going, too. We found out today that I got the assistant job. If I hadn't been hired, I would have stayed home this summer and continued to look for work here."

"Maybe Steven's aunt has other plans for the summer. Maybe she's going on a trip herself."

"Aunt Ethel doesn't travel anymore," Steven said.

I envisioned a frail old woman in a rocking chair.

I left the house, got my bike out of the garage, and rode off, pedaling as hard as I could. Anger formed a hard knot in my chest. Why should I get shipped off to spend the summer with an elderly woman I'd never met?

I didn't blame Steven; I blamed Mom. Steven had to go where his company sent him, but Mom had a choice. She could stay home this summer if she wanted to. She could look for a job here and let me play summer baseball.

I rode until my legs ached and ribbons of sweat rolled down my face. When I returned home, I went straight upstairs, got in the shower, and let the water pour over my head, wishing it could wash away my problems. I was sorry I'd made the team. If I had been cut, I would've been glad to leave town for the summer.

I dressed and sat on my bed, still fuming. There was a knock on the bedroom door.

"May I come in?" Mom asked.

I sighed.

"Josh, we need to talk."

"Okay, okay. Come in."

Mom sat beside me. "I've tried hard to find a job here," she said. "I'm registered with several employment agencies, I read the Help Wanted ads every day, and I've sent out dozens of applications and résumés. I wish I had found work but I haven't, and we need the money. This is my chance to contribute to our income, and it might lead to a permanent job. Please try to understand."

I stared at my shoes. I understood why Mom wanted to go, but that didn't help me any.

"Why do I have to go live with a stranger?" I said. "If I can't stay here, why can't I go back to Vermont where my friends are and spend the summer with Gramma?"

"Gramma's having hip surgery the first of June,"

Mom said. "She'll be laid up much of the summer."

"I could take care of her."

"She'll need help bathing and dressing for a while. Aunt Marian is going to stay with her."

There was no sense arguing. With Mom's sister in Gramma's spare bedroom, there wasn't any place for me. I knew I couldn't stay with my dad, either. He's in the Army, so my visits with him are restricted to when he's on leave. My summer in Washington was a done deal, and I could do nothing to change it.

I wondered what Steven's aunt was like. What if Aunt Ethel was an old fuddy-duddy who expected me to have perfect manners and listen to opera and wear a necktie? She didn't travel, which meant she wasn't adventuresome. I figured I'd be bored out of my mind.

Now, lying in bed on my first night in Aunt Ethel's house, I knew I'd been wrong about that. Aunt Ethel was definitely not boring.

Mom had packed paper and pens, as well as envelopes, already stamped and addressed. The last thing she had said to me was "Be sure to write!"

I had not expected to write often because I didn't think there would be anything interesting to report. Now I clicked the light on, found my notebook and pen, and wrote a letter.

June 15

Dear Mom and Steven,

Did you know that a bullet makes a whizzing sound as it flies past your head? I found that out in person, and I hope I never hear the sound again.

When Aunt Ethel and I got home tonight, we saw a bat flying around in the house. Aunt Ethel does not like bats, so she got out a shotgun and chased after it. I told her not to kill it, but she pulled the trigger anyway. I'm glad I wasn't standing any closer. My ears rang for an hour.

She hit the bat, and it fell down behind a cupboard. We couldn't get it out, so now it's rotting back there.

Aunt Ethel baked a cake for me, but we had to throw it out because it had bat blood all over it.

Your nervous son,
Josh

P.S. I can't wear a seat belt because Aunt Ethel's truck doesn't have them. It doesn't matter; the way Aunt Ethel drives, even a seat belt won't save me.

I knew that bat blood, bullets, and no seat belts would give Mom fits, but I didn't care. She's the one who had made me come here.

I fell asleep hoping the hotel in India was full of spiders.

CHAPTER THREE

I awoke to a horrible scream. Heart pounding, I jumped out of bed and rushed to the window, certain I would see either Aunt Ethel's murderer making his getaway or a scene fit for *National Geographic*, where a cougar catches an antelope and dismembers it.

Early sunlight filtered through the forest; the trees stretched calmly into the distance. I saw no murderer. No cougar. Except for a few birds fluttering between the trees, there was no movement of any kind.

The scream sounded again. It pierced the morning air, even more shrill than when Aunt Ethel first saw the bat. This time I realized it came from the front side of the house, outside the living room.

I pulled on shorts and a sweatshirt, then ran downstairs. Aunt Ethel stood in the kitchen, calmly stirring something in a big pot on the stove. It smelled like spaghetti sauce.

"What's happening?" I asked. "Who's screaming?"

"Oh, that's Florence. I should have warned you. I'm so used to her, I never gave it a thought."

Speechless, I looked at my hostess, who wore the same pink dress she'd had on the night before. I decided I was right about it being her nightgown.

I went to the living room and cautiously peeked out a window.

A large peacock perched on the front-porch rail, its turquoise feathers shimmering in the sunlight. Gray glops the size of silver dollars dotted the porch floor beneath the rail. Yuck. Seeing them made me uneasy. Compared to this peacock mess, bat droppings were practically invisible. I hoped Aunt Ethel didn't get out her gun.

As I watched the peacock, it called out again.

I had never before heard a peacock cry. How could something so beautiful make such a shrill, ugly noise? It sounded as if it were being tortured, but there it sat, calm as you please, on the porch rail.

Aunt Ethel strode toward the door, motioning for me to follow her. She stepped out to the porch, set a pan of cracked corn on the porch floor, and said,

"Good morning, Florence." The peacock hopped down and began to eat.

I edged out the door to watch, being careful where I put my bare feet.

"This is our great-nephew, Josh McDowell," Aunt Ethel told the bird. "His stepdad is Will's boy, Steven. Josh will be staying with us for the summer, the way Steven used to."

The crown of feathers on the bird's head bobbed up and down as he pecked at the corn.

Aunt Ethel smiled at me. "This is your Aunt Florence," she said. "My sister."

The peacock continued its breakfast.

"Your—sister?" I waited for Aunt Ethel to explain.

"Florence was three years older than I," Aunt Ethel said. "We were the youngest and the only girls in a family of six children, so we were always close. Since neither of us married, we lived together here in the family home after our parents were gone. My brothers are gone now, too. Florence loved birds, and she told me many times that after she died, she planned to come back as a peacock, the most beautiful bird of all."

A chill shivered up the back of my neck. I vaguely

remembered Steven mentioning that there used to be an Aunt Florence on his long-ago summer visits.

"Florence passed away last January," Aunt Ethel said. "In March, I woke one morning to find a peacock on my porch, and Florence has been here ever since."

"Isn't this a male bird?" I asked. "I thought only the males had those bright tail feathers."

"You're right," Aunt Ethel said. "Only the males are peacocks; the females are peahens. The males have the long, beautiful feathers, called trains. Some of Florence's train feathers are nearly six feet long!"

"They're beautiful," I said. "The spots on them look like eyes."

As if he knew we were admiring him, the peacock spread his train into a huge fan and strutted around the porch.

"If I were going to return as a peafowl, I'd be a male," Aunt Ethel said. "Wouldn't you?"

"I guess so."

"All right, then," Aunt Ethel said, as if that ended the matter.

I wondered whether Aunt Ethel had ever advertised that she'd found a peacock. This bird seemed tame; it must be a lost pet. Someone had probably been looking for their peacock for the last three months.

I didn't ask because I knew Aunt Ethel wanted to believe the peacock was her sister. I wondered if Mom and Steven knew about the peacock. I was pretty sure they didn't, and I could hardly wait to tell them.

I began planning a second letter. I'd say I wasn't sure if Aunt Ethel belonged to some odd religious cult or if she was plain losing her marbles.

"Are you ready for breakfast?"

"Sure." I was always ready for breakfast.

"We have a special treat today from my friend's garden: young peas, still in the pod. Florence and I used to stand in the garden and eat peas as soon as we picked them. That's how they're best, uncooked. I can't keep up a garden anymore, but my friend, Muriel, knows how I love fresh peas so she brought these yesterday."

Raw peas? For breakfast? Oh, great, I thought. She's a health food nut. I'll eat nothing but Brussels sprouts and cauliflower all summer and go home so malnourished I'll never be able to lift a baseball bat again.

I followed Aunt Ethel to the kitchen.

"I hope you like spaghetti," she said. "It's too much trouble to make only for myself."

"I love spaghetti, but I've never had it for breakfast."

"One of the good things about living alone," Aunt Ethel said, "is that I can eat whatever I want, anytime I want it. Spaghetti is one of my favorite breakfasts."

She handed me a plate. A pile of raw peas, still in the pods, rose beside the spaghetti and meat sauce. "I eat fresh fruit or veggies with every meal," Aunt Ethel said. "That's the secret of my long life. Raw vegetables and fruits are packed with nutrients."

I knew she was probably right, but if I could eat anything I wanted at any time, I wouldn't choose raw peas for breakfast.

Aunt Ethel picked up a pea pod, held it lengthwise between her thumb and forefinger, and pressed until the pod made a *snap* sound. It split open, revealing a row of green peas. Using her thumb, Aunt Ethel pushed the peas into her palm, then popped them in her mouth.

I picked up a pea pod and snapped it open. I put one of the peas in my mouth. I'd never eaten a raw pea before; it was crunchy and sweet.

"It's good," I said. I emptied the pod and ate the peas.

Aunt Ethel beamed. "Do you want Parmesan on your spaghetti?"

Nodding, I reached for a shaker of Parmesan cheese.

Aunt Ethel split another pea pod, expertly sliding the peas into her palm. "What are your plans for the day?"

I knew what I wished I could do that day: go to baseball practice, hang out with some of the guys afterward, maybe rent a movie. Longing for home brought a lump to my throat.

I looked down at my plate. "I don't know. What did you do in the summertime when you were my age?" I asked.

"Florence and I weeded the garden and helped with the canning. If we had any free time, we played in our tree house."

"Steven mentioned the tree house. Is it still there?"

"As far as I know, it is. I haven't walked in the woods for years, but if it stood up to all of us children, plus those in the second generation, it's probably still standing. Florence and I called it our deer-watching station. We made a pact not to talk while we were there until after we'd seen at least one deer. We used to take picnic lunches until Florence decided the tree house was haunted. Then she refused to go there anymore, and it wasn't fun to look for deer alone, so I quit going, too."

"What made her think the tree house was haunted?"

"Lawsy, child, Florence was full of fanciful ideas. She'd take a notion into her head, and there was no changing her mind, whether it made sense or not."

Kind of like deciding your dead sister came back as a peacock, I thought. Gramma always said people believe what they want to be true, regardless of the facts. Aunt Ethel's peacock seemed to prove Gramma's theory.

This morning Aunt Ethel didn't look wild-eyed, as she had when she chased the bat. She looked weary, and I realized my presence for two months was probably as difficult for her as it was for me. I wondered how early she had gotten up to cook spaghetti sauce.

When I offered to wash the breakfast dishes, Aunt Ethel gratefully accepted. "I overdid it last night," she said. "I'm not used to climbing ladders or scrubbing the floor on my knees. Usually I only need to sweep. My muscles ache today."

I was glad to hear last night's bat episode had not been business as usual.

Aunt Ethel didn't have a dishwasher—no surprise—so I filled the sink with warm sudsy water and began swishing our plates around while my thoughts drifted back home. With the two-hour time difference, the summer league team was probably practicing right then. I wondered who was playing right field.

Minneapolis seemed far, far away, not only in miles but also in lifestyle. Mall of America sells all the latest fashions and electronic equipment, none of which seemed necessary here. When I got off the bus in Carbon City, it was as if I'd stepped back in time fifty years.

When I finished the dishes, I wrote another letter.

June 16
Dear Mom and Steven,

I woke up early today because I heard screaming from the front porch. I thought for sure Aunt Ethel was being murdered, but it turned out to be a peacock. If you've never heard the noise a peacock makes, consider yourself lucky. I won't need an alarm clock this summer; the peacock wakes half the county.

Now here's the eerie part: Aunt Ethel thinks the peacock is Aunt Florence! She truly believes her dead sister has come back as a peacock. She calls the bird Florence and

talks to it as if it knew all the family history.
It gives me the creeps.

> *Your anxious son,*
> *Josh*

As I reread my two letters, I hoped my language-arts teacher next fall would ask us to write a paper about "What I Did On My Summer Vacation." Between the dead bat and the screaming peacock, I'd get an *A* for sure, even if I did nothing else for the rest of the summer.

As it turned out, what I did next was even more weird than watching a bat get shot indoors or meeting a peacock who's supposed to be my dead great-aunt, and those were hard acts to follow.

I soon found out Florence had been right about the tree house being haunted. That's when my summer really got exciting—and dangerous.

CHAPTER FOUR

"Which direction is the tree house?" I asked when I had finished writing my second letter.

Aunt Ethel pointed. "There used to be a path," she said, "but it's overgrown now. Wear long pants in the woods; the berry vines grab your legs. There's a compass hanging on the back porch. Take it along. It's easy to get turned around in the trees until you learn your way."

I changed into jeans, then went out the kitchen door. A small compass on a shoelace dangled from a nail. I put the looped shoelace over my head, wondering who had worn it last and how long ago.

Mom had worried about me being in the woods alone this summer and had suggested buying me a cell phone. Steven had said, "It would be a waste of money; there's no cell service out there."

At the time, I'd thought it was an excuse not to get me a phone, but as I looked around at the unspoiled forest, I knew he was right. There was no point building a cellular tower in a place where hardly anyone lived. Add cellular phone service to the long list of things Carbon City doesn't have.

I headed into the grove of trees behind Aunt Ethel's house. Steven had told me Aunt Ethel owned about fifty acres, which sounded like a lot. Maybe I'd see deer or squirrels. I planned to search for the old tree house. If I found it, I intended to carry some of my books out there. A tree house would be the perfect place to read—far from Aunt Florence's screams.

I glanced back at the house. It had seemed so gloomy last night, but now the sunshine gave it a cheerful look, despite its peeling paint. Bright yellow daisies bloomed along the foundation, and white petals drifted down from a large flowering tree near the back door.

As the woods closed behind me, I noted I was headed east. No matter how peaceful the woods were, or how much wildlife I spotted, I wanted to be sure I could find my way out.

I picked my way through the undergrowth, inhaling the smell of fir and cedar. I wished Aunt Ethel had a dog. This would be the perfect place for a dog to run, sniffing at the fallen trees, searching out rabbits or mice to chase.

Charlie would have loved it here. In my imagination, I saw Charlie's short dachshund legs scrambling through the bushes, his nose leading the way to adventure.

You were a good dog, Charlie, I thought, the best dog ever. I miss you.

Why did Charlie have to get mouth cancer when he was only nine years old? Why did . . .

I snipped off the thought before it could grow. Mom had said, "Remember the happy times with Charlie, and forget the end of the story. The only way to survive the loss of someone you love is to remember the good times."

With my thoughts on Charlie, I forgot to watch for deer. The sudden snap of a branch breaking startled me, and I glanced toward the sound.

A beautiful doe stood about ten yards away, watching me. We looked at each other for a few seconds, then the deer bounded off, flashing her black tail.

Ten minutes later, I spotted the tree house. I had

expected a rickety platform balanced in the branches of a large tree, but I found a sturdy wooden structure, enclosed on all four sides, with a sloping roof of corrugated tin.

It wasn't literally a tree house, because it wasn't attached to a tree. It rested on four unpeeled logs, each about eight inches in diameter, set in concrete. The building stood ten feet off the ground, completely surrounded by huge fir trees. A wooden ladder leaned against the narrow platform outside the tree-house door.

I stood on the bottom rung of the ladder, testing it. Then I climbed quickly to the platform and pushed open the door. The tree house was eight feet square with windows on three sides—not glass windows, but rectangles cut from the walls, with shutters that closed to keep the rain out. I imagined a young Aunt Ethel and her sister silently gazing out the windows while they waited for deer.

Dry leaves crunched underfoot on the floor, and cobwebs crisscrossed the window openings. A small makeshift table built of four pieces of log and a plank squatted in one corner.

I liked the tree house. After I gave it a thorough sweeping and brought out a chair, it would be a perfect spot to read and listen to music. Maybe I would bring lunch here, too, or at least a snack to eat while I watched for wildlife.

I hurried back to the house for a broom and a damp rag to clean the table. Aunt Ethel, pleased I had found the tree house, gave me an oversized pillow to take there for the summer. "It's the same pillow Steven used in the tree house," she said.

I swept and scrubbed, then went back for some cheese and crackers and my box of books. With all three windows open, the tree house had plenty of light to read by. I sank onto the pillow and opened a book.

I was deep into a mystery novel when a faint sound caught my attention. Another deer? I put down my book, moved quietly to the window, and peered out. I waited, listening, my eyes scanning the trees for movement.

"Meow."

I looked toward the sound. A scrawny cat sat in the woods, its brown-and-tan-striped fur blending into the background.

"Hello, kitty."

The startled cat hurried away.

I broke off a piece of cheese and dropped it out the window. I waited.

Soon the cat returned, moving cautiously. He sniffed the cheese, then gulped it down.

I tossed out another piece. The cat backed away from the tree house, looking up at the window. When I remained still, the cat edged forward again and gobbled up the cheese.

The poor thing is starving, I thought. I broke the rest of my cheese into pieces and dropped them to the ground. The cat ate it all, then looked up as if hoping for more, but he didn't meow again. I wondered why the cat had meowed in the first place. Had he smelled the cheese from so far away? Or had he smelled me and taken a chance that I would feed him?

When the cheese was gone, the cat washed his whiskers, then turned and went into the woods. He walked slowly and looked back once before he vanished into the undergrowth.

I put a bookmark in my book and laid the book on the floor beside the pillow. I closed the shutters on the windows, climbed down the ladder, and hurried home.

The house smelled like chocolate. Aunt Ethel stood in the kitchen, frosting a layer cake.

"That smells wonderful," I said.

"It's your new Welcome cake. Did you see any deer?"

"Yes, and I saw a starving cat."

"Fleas and mosquitoes! Not another stray."

"I fed him some of my cheese."

"Oh, don't do that again. Feed a stray cat, and it'll hang around forever."

"He was hungry."

"Plenty of mice in the woods."

"He acted scared, and he didn't have a collar on. Do you have anything I can feed him, like a can of tuna?"

"No. I don't cotton much to cats. Florence was the one with the soft heart for critters—always feeding some stray cat or taking in a lost dog. People dump animals out here, you know. Put them right at the end of my driveway and hope they'll live in the woods."

I wondered if someone had dumped a peacock.

"Would you drive me to Carbon City?" I asked. "The Market might sell cat food."

Aunt Ethel swirled her knife through the frosting, smoothing it across the cake's top. "Feeding that cat is not a good idea."

"Mom says we should be kind to all creatures and help them when we can."

"It wouldn't be a kindness to make a cat dependent on you for its food. You'll leave at summer's end, and the cat will starve."

"By then maybe I can find someone who wants to adopt him."

"I don't want a cat coming around, bothering Florence."

I realized Aunt Ethel didn't want to help the cat because she feared it would hurt the peacock.

"I could feed it out by the tree house," I said.

"It would follow you home."

I looked away, annoyed by her lack of caring. First she killed an innocent bat, and now she refused to help a starving cat. The Welcome cake looked delicious, but I couldn't enjoy cake when the cat needed food. There had to be some way to help. "Is there a humane society or other group that rescues strays?" I asked.

"We tried to build an animal shelter once," Aunt Ethel said, "so there'd be a good place to take the unwanted dogs and cats. Everyone got together— all the small towns around here—and we had a big auction. It was the most exciting event we ever had in these parts, let me tell you. Businesses donated expensive items for the auction—trips, and a new car, even two tickets to the World Series."

"Wow! I'd like to win that."

"Children held bake sales and car washes and put decorated collection cans in all the stores. Lots of folks contributed. Florence and I gave five hundred dollars, in memory of our parents. Altogether, the community raised one hundred thirty thousand dollars for the shelter. It should have been built by now, but it isn't going to happen."

"Why not?"

"Someone stole all the money."

"Stole it! How?"

"The day of the auction, all the coins were put in one of those coin-counting machines and then exchanged for large bills, which were taken to the auction. It was called "Cash for Critters," and those who attended the auction were asked to pay in cash. It was a gimmick, to see how high the pile of money would be, and it worked. One of the TV stations from Seattle even sent a reporter to film it. People got all fired up when they saw that heap of money grow bigger, and some even threw bills on the pile without bidding. After the auction, the county treasurer and the auction chairman counted the money. Then they put it in bags and took it to the bank's night deposit."

Tears sprang to Aunt Ethel's eyes. "Before the money could be deposited, an armed robber stole it all."

"No! How? What happened?"

"As the two men walked from their car to the night deposit, a man wearing a ski mask and dark clothing jumped around the corner of the bank with a gun pointed at them. He grabbed the bags of money and fled. His car was parked out of sight, and he was in it and gone before they could get a license plate number."

"He never got caught?"

Aunt Ethel shook her head, no. "Mr. Turlep, the bank manager, posted a reward for information leading to an arrest, but it didn't help. The money was never found."

"Doesn't the bank have insurance?"

"Not for money that was never deposited. For a long time we hoped the robber would be caught and the money would be recovered. When we realized it wasn't going to happen, there was talk of starting over and doing the auction again, but most folks had run out of steam by then. We'd given generously already; it was hard to get excited about doing it over again, and many folks couldn't afford to give twice."

The story made me angry. Aunt Ethel would have to bake a lot of cakes to earn five hundred dollars. She'd given a donation out of love, as a way to honor her parents, and some scumbag had stolen it.

"So we never got our animal shelter," she said, "and people still dump unwanted cats and dogs in the woods."

"Maybe if I feed the stray cat, I can tame it and then we can find a home for it. There may not be a shelter to help all the animals, but we could help this one."

"No. Cats kill birds."

"The peacock—Florence—is way bigger than the cat."

"Florence." She paused, then smiled. "I've been thinking," she said. "Ever since you asked what I did as a child, my mind's brimmed with memories. Florence and I used to ride our bicycles down to Carbon City to buy penny candy. We had a big tire that we hung from the chestnut tree with a rope; it made a fine swing. We played marbles, too, and hop-scotch, and in the evening when our brothers finished dinner, we all played kick-the-can."

She had a faraway look, as if she saw her sister and brothers still hiding behind trees, waiting to dash out to kick the tin can. She'd forgotten all about the stolen money and the stray cat.

"I think that big tire is still in the barn," she said. "Maybe you'd like to hang it in the tree this summer."

"I'll go look for it," I said, not because I cared about the swing but because I was upset that Aunt Ethel wouldn't let me feed the cat. Right then, I wanted to get away from her. I felt sorry about the shelter money and sorry all her family had died, but I also felt sorry for the dead bat and the hungry stray cat.

I walked across the yard to the barn, then lifted the wooden bar that held the door shut. The air inside smelled like stale bread. Dust motes drifted in the shaft of sunlight that followed me through the door. A small, unseen critter scuttled away.

Old rakes, shovels, and other garden implements lined up beside the door. I'd seen similar tools in Vermont, when Mom and I browsed in antiques shops.

I didn't see the tire, but I spotted two old bicycles, one blue and one red, leaning against the far wall. The blue bike had two flat tires. The red bike's tires still held air. I grabbed the handlebars and walked the red bike out of the barn. I mounted it and pushed off, pedaling across the grass.

At home I had a ten-speed bike with narrow tires and hand brakes. These tires were much wider, and I had to practice braking with my feet. After I had the hang of it, I went inside.

"I found a bike in the barn," I said. "Is it OK if I go for a bike ride?" I hoped she wouldn't ask where I planned to go.

"Watch for cars," Aunt Ethel said.

I promised to be careful.

Before I left, I went up to my room and took a ten-dollar bill from the money Mom and Steven had given me. "You'll need spending money," Steven had said, "in case you go to town. If there's nothing else you want, you can always buy ice-cream bars at the Carbon City Market."

Or cat food, I thought, as I stuffed the money into my pocket. If Aunt Ethel used to ride a bike to Carbon City and back, I could do it, too.

CHAPTER FIVE

Clutching the handlebars, I flew down the hill. The road had no bike lane, but it didn't matter because there weren't any cars, either. I stayed on the edge of the road, listening for approaching vehicles. I coasted much of the time, braking when the bike started going too fast.

I rolled into Carbon City and stopped where the bus had dropped me off. At home, I always put a chain and padlock on my bike when I left it. Here I put the kickstand down and walked into the Carbon City Market.

An elderly man sat behind the small counter, reading a magazine. He looked up when I entered, nodded, and returned to his reading.

Shelves lined both side walls of the Market, with two rows of merchandise in the middle. A cooler for milk and soft drinks and a small freezer faced forward from the back wall. With no produce or meat, people wouldn't do a weekly grocery shopping here, but the locals could stop by to pick up what they forgot in town or to buy snack items such as candy and popcorn.

One area in the front looked like a mini-hardware store, with tools, electrical cords, and a bin of nails.

Mostly the store sold the kinds of items people run out of: bathroom tissue, orange juice, canned fruits and vegetables, flour, and sugar. I found cat food along the right-hand wall.

I almost missed it because I was looking for a big bag; the store had only one-pound boxes. I knew it probably cost more this way, but I carried a box to the counter.

"Haven't seen you before," the man said as he gave me my change.

"I'm visiting for the summer."

I could tell he wanted to ask who I was visiting, but I didn't give him a chance. I figured in a town like this everyone knew everyone else, and I didn't want word to get back to Aunt Ethel that I had been in Carbon City buying cat food.

"Could I have a bag, please?" I said.

He put the box of cat food in a blue plastic bag

that said WAL-MART on it. He must save bags from his own shopping to reuse in the store.

"Thanks," I said, and hurried out.

I hung the bag on the handlebars and headed back to Aunt Ethel's house. I had sailed down the hill, but I crawled back up. I kept wanting to shift the bike to a lower gear, the way I would at home. Instead, I stood up and pumped until my leg muscles ached, my damp T-shirt clung to my back, and my breath came in short gasps. If I did this a couple of times a week, I'd be in great shape by the end of summer. Part of the time I had to dismount and walk the bike up the steep hill.

Finally I turned down Aunt Ethel's gravel driveway.

As I returned the bike to the barn, I planned my next move. I decided to keep the cat food in the tree house. It would be where I needed it, and Aunt Ethel would not discover it.

Ordinarily I would have felt guilty about doing something I had been told not to do, but I felt too sorry for the cat to be remorseful. If I didn't help the cat, who would? The cat's hunger seemed more important than following Aunt Ethel's rules. If I only fed it out by the tree house, it wouldn't bother Florence.

Leaving the cat food in the barn, I went inside. The house was quiet. Aunt Ethel lay tilted back in her recliner, snoring softly. I splashed some cold water on my face and filled a glass. As I drank, I realized the cat would need water as well as food.

Earlier, when I put away the breakfast dishes, I had seen some small plastic bowls with snap-on lids. Now I helped myself to two of the bowls. I filled one with water and snapped a lid on it, then went back to the barn to retrieve the box of cat food.

When I reached the tree house, I opened the bowl of water and shook cat food into the other bowl. I left both bowls on the ground, where the cheese had landed. Then I climbed up the ladder to wait for Mr. Stray. Of course, I didn't know for sure if the cat was male or female, but I wanted to name him something. Mr. Stray seemed appropriate.

I wondered where he slept. I hoped no coyotes or cougars prowled the woods at night.

I stayed at the window for ten minutes or so. Twice I called, "Here, kitty, kitty," in case Mr. Stray had once been a pet and would know to come when called. There was no sign of the cat.

As I watched, I felt myself relax. It seemed peaceful in the woods. No traffic noise, no boom boxes blaring, no kids at play or parents calling the kids to come home. Nothing here but Mother Nature at her best.

I decided to read while I waited. If I looked outside before I turned the page each time, I wouldn't miss Mr. Stray. I settled onto the pillow and reached for my book. It was not where I had left it.

I'd placed it on the floor beside my pillow. Now it lay under the table.

Someone's been here, I thought. Someone came in the tree house while I was away. Who? No neighbors lived nearby. A transient?

I checked the box of crackers I had left on the table. I'd rolled the inner wrapper tightly so I wouldn't attract mice or ants. The crackers were exactly as I'd left them; the box was still half full. Surely a transient would have eaten them.

Someone bent on mischief would have vandalized the tree house, but everything was tidy. If the book had not been moved, I would never have guessed anyone had been here.

The thought of an intruder made me uneasy. If someone came in here once, they might come again. The feeling of peace and solitude vanished. I felt edgy and kept listening for approaching footsteps.

Why would someone move my book—to let me know he'd been here?

Maybe I hadn't put the book on the floor; maybe I remembered it wrong. That must be it, I decided. I forgot where I'd left the book earlier.

I opened the book, but I couldn't concentrate on the story. After a few minutes, I replaced my bookmark and set the book down, paying attention to exactly where I placed it: on the floor beside the pillow.

When I looked out a window, I saw Mr. Stray hunched over the water bowl, lapping up the water. I felt glad that I had brought it for him.

After he finished drinking, he ate some cat food. As I watched, I thought, I'm going to try to tame him. If I can get him used to me, maybe Mom will let me keep him. I could get a cat carrier and take him home on the plane.

"Hello, Mr. Stray," I whispered. Instantly, he fled into the bushes. I waited, not moving. After a few minutes, he crept back to the food.

I let him eat a while before I said, "Hello, Mr. Stray" again. He looked up, froze, and then, after staring at me for a few seconds, he cautiously began eating again. "Good kitty," I whispered. "Good Mr. Stray." That time he didn't bother to look.

I'll get him used to my voice, I thought. He'll start

to associate my voice with food, and he won't be afraid of me.

When he finished, he washed his whiskers again, then stood and stretched before he went back into the woods.

I climbed down the ladder, refilled the cat food bowl, and turned to leave. Mr. Stray stood on a big rock, watching me. I sat cross-legged on the ground next to the food and water. I watched him, but I didn't say anything. After a few minutes, he stepped off the rock and walked away into the woods.

Encouraged that he let me be so close, I began planning how I could keep him. If he was tame, I thought Mom would let me take him home, even if it cost extra on the plane. By now she and Steven were probably feeling so guilty about ruining my summer, they would agree to letting me have a cat.

Meanwhile I should take Mr. Stray to a veterinarian as soon as I could. I knew from taking care of Charlie that animals must be wormed and neutered. Mr. Stray also had to be vaccinated for rabies and whatever else cats get. I had no idea how I would manage to transport him to a vet. I couldn't carry him on a bicycle, that's for sure. I would have to try to change Aunt Ethel's mind about helping him. Of course, I had to catch him first.

Pleased by my success in getting close to Mr. Stray, I decided to stay at the tree house a while. I felt like reading now.

I climbed the ladder, savoring the silence again. I knew my afternoons in the tree house, alone with my books, would be the best part of the summer. Except for helping Mr. Stray, of course.

I entered the tree house, opened the windows, flopped onto my pillow, and reached for the book. It wasn't where I'd left it.

I looked around, all my senses alert now. What was going on here? This time I was positive where I'd put the book. No one could possibly have come in the tree house while I sat with Mr. Stray; the ladder had been in plain sight. Yet the book lay on the table, along with two others from the box. A feeling of foreboding prickled the hairs on the back of my neck.

I stuck my head out each of the windows, searching the woods for any sign of another person. I saw only the woods, heard only the chirping of the birds and the low hum of a small airplane engine in the distance.

Shaken, I decided to take my book back to the house and read it there.

I hurried home, glancing often over my shoulder. I wondered what had made Aunt Florence think the tree house was haunted. I could ask Aunt Ethel, but I didn't want to tell her about the book. She might refuse to let me go back to the tree house, and I wanted to keep feeding Mr. Stray.

I tried to act nonchalant when I went inside. Aunt Ethel was still in her recliner, but she was awake and reading a cookbook.

I got a drink of water, then went up to my room, lay on the bed, and tried to read. I couldn't concentrate, though. For the first time ever, my own life was more mysterious and interesting than the book I was partway through. I put it down and thought about everything that had happened since I got to Carbon City.

Was it wrong to feed the cat when Aunt Ethel had said not to? Or was it worse to ignore an animal's hunger when I could help it? Should I tell Aunt Ethel about the book being moved? I knew I wasn't mistaken about that; it had really been moved, but by whom? Should I mail the letters I'd written, knowing they would make Mom and Steven worry? I had plenty of questions but no answers.

After a while I went downstairs.

"Where did you go on your bike ride?" Aunt Ethel asked.

"Down the hill toward Carbon City. It was easier

going down than coming back up." That wasn't the whole truth, but it wasn't a lie, either.

She laughed. "I could have told you that." She passed me a bowl of raw baby carrots. "Snack time."

I took a few carrots to munch on. "Is there anything you want me to do for you?" I asked. I expected her to hand me a dust cloth or a broom or maybe suggest I pull some weeds.

"Do you know how to knit?" she asked.

Knit? "Um, no, I don't."

"I'll teach you. I'm knitting a scarf as a gift for Muriel, but I have arthritis in my hands, and it's getting too hard to work the knitting needles. I only have a few inches left to do."

She opened a large shopping bag and withdrew a scarf about two feet long in shades of purple, lavender, and red. One end of the scarf hung on a wooden knitting needle whose pointed end was stuck through a big ball of yarn. A second needle was also stuck in the yarn.

Aunt Ethel sat on the couch, patting the cushion beside her to indicate where I should sit. I sat. She showed me how to hold the knitting needles, how to stick the point of the empty needle into the end stitch on the other needle, then loop the yarn over and slide the stitch off the first needle, where the scarf was, and onto the other needle. It didn't look hard, but when I tried, I felt as if I had ten thumbs. Gradually, I got the hang of it with Aunt Ethel giving me directions every step of the way.

"While you do that," she said, "I'll start our dinner. We're having oatmeal pancakes with applesauce."

Spaghetti for breakfast and pancakes for dinner.

Knit one, knit two. If the guys on the summer baseball team could see me now, I thought, they'd fall over laughing. When I write the paper on my summer vacation, I think I'll leave out the part about learning to knit.

After a while, though, I began to enjoy the repetitive motion and the clicking of the knitting needles. Once I didn't have to concentrate so hard on how to do it, I found the process relaxing, and I let my mind drift to the tree house and the question of who, or what, had been there with me.

Although I had been frightened when I left, I decided to return first thing the next morning. I had to go back to feed Mr. Stray, but now I also wanted to see if any of the books got moved overnight. Maybe the tree house was still haunted, as Aunt Florence had believed it was seventy years ago.

CHAPTER SIX

My first thought when I awoke the next morning was: I wonder if any books were moved around in the night. I dressed quickly and hurried downstairs.

Breakfast was pork chops, green beans, fried potatoes, and the leftover applesauce from the oatmeal pancakes. I was glad that the beans were cooked.

I washed the dishes quickly, then headed for the tree house again. I took the book I'd brought home the day before and carefully placed it on the table. Then I went back down the ladder to refill Mr. Stray's bowl.

I didn't see the cat, nor did I hear any movement in the woods. No deer, no squirrels.

Back in the tree house, I looked out each of the windows, my eyes searching for Mr. Stray. When I didn't see him, I reached for a different book, one that I had left there overnight.

As I picked it up, a voice from behind me said, "You won't like the ending."

I dropped the book and whirled toward the man's voice, my heart thumping.

He peered in at me through one of the windows. He must have moved the ladder—which meant I couldn't climb down now and run away. Why hadn't I seen him when I was feeding Mr. Stray? How could I not have heard the ladder being moved?

"The horse dies," he continued. "I don't like books where the animal dies at the end. Why can't them writers figure out a better way to tell a story than to kill the poor horse?"

"Who are you?" I whispered.

His eyes lit up, and a huge grin spread across his face. "You can hear me?" he asked.

I nodded.

"Can you see me, too?"

"Yes." Why wouldn't I?

"Hee-haw!" The man yelped like a cowboy starting into the rodeo ring.

I backed toward the door.

He's crazy, I thought. He's a delusional escaped mental patient. I'll have to jump from the door to the ground, hope I don't break a bone, and try to out-run him.

"I thank you for the loan of your books," he said. "Never owned a book myself. 'Course, I didn't learn to read until after I died."

My scalp prickled with apprehension. *After he died?*

"Still can hardly believe I'd be glad for book learn-ing," the man said. "I quit going to school when I was seven years old in order to stay home and help with farm chores, and I left with no regrets. The only parts of school I liked were lunch and recess. I played hooky half the time and ignored my lessons the other half. Never thought I'd know how to read. I didn't learn for the rest of my life but since then, well, I have a natural curiosity, and after I died, I started spend-ing my nights in the library. Being around so many books, I naturally opened one here and there to look at the pictures, and then one night I opened a book that had pictures of coal mines, and I started figuring out the words, and once I got the hang of it, I never stopped. Since they closed the Carbon City Library, back in 1964, I don't get many chances to read."

As he talked, I slid my feet closer to the door. I hardly heard what he said. How had he moved the ladder so quickly? Only a few seconds had passed between when I'd looked out the window and when he looked in.

"Don't go running off," he said. "I ain't had anyone to talk to in more than fifty years."

Keeping my eyes on the face in the window, I felt behind me until my hand touched the door. I shoved it open and saw the ladder right where I had left it. What was the man standing on?

"Nothing to be scared of," the man said. "I ain't armed, if that's what you're thinking, and I wouldn't hurt you anyway. You're the first friendly soul I've met in decades."

Friendly? I was trying my best to get away from this nutcase, and he thought I was acting friendly.

"I wouldn't take the life of a boy, that's certain," he said. "Unlike some folks I know, I value a human life."

His voice had an angry edge now, as if he were talking about a specific incident. I decided it would be best to change the subject and calm him down before I tried to escape.

"Do you live around here?" I asked.

"Used to. Do you mind if I come in?"

Since he'd already been in the tree house at least twice, I figured I couldn't stop him even if I wanted to so I said, "OK," and the next thing I knew he was standing near the little table. He didn't climb in the open window; he simply materialized inside the tree house. One second he was a face at the window, and the next second he stood beside me.

I gasped. He must be a ghost! How else could he float through the wall that way? All his talk of learning to read after he died made sense, if he was a ghost.

I stared at my visitor. I'd always thought ghosts were delicate, transparent beings that a living person could see through, but this man was as solid as a tree stump. If I had not seen him go from outside to inside the tree house like magic, I would never have suspected he wasn't a flesh-and-blood person.

"Why are you here?" I asked. "Who are you?"

"Name's Wilber," he said. "Wilber Martin, but everyone called me Willie. I'm an angel."

Unkempt hair framed his face. He wore a grubby gray work shirt, an odd hat with some kind of light on the front of it, and one sturdy high-top boot. His right pant leg was pinned up above the knee.

This angel needed a shave.

"You don't look like an angel," I said.

"How do you know? Have you met other angels?"

"No, but I always thought angels wore long white gowns and had shiny wings and halos."

"Ha! That's a stereotype, if ever I heard one.

Angels aren't all the same, just as people aren't all the same."

"An angel should look kindly, like Cinderella's fairy godmother in the Disney movie."

"Cinderella? Disney?"

I could tell he had no idea what I was talking about. Maybe he really was an angel. What did I know about angels?

Whoever or whatever he was, he didn't seem to be a threat. My heart quit thundering in my chest, and my breathing returned to normal. Part of me still wanted to scramble down the ladder and run, but another part of me overflowed with curiosity. I stayed next to the door, ready to bolt if I needed to, but I kept talking to the man/ghost and listening to what he said.

"Tell me about yourself," I said.

"Not much to tell. What do you want to know?"

"How did you lose your leg?"

"In a mining accident. Got caught in the explosion of nineteen-oh-three. My leg's buried in the Carbon City cemetery. My brother made a proper little casket for it, like you'd put a baby in. He said a Bible verse, and my wife sang a hymn, and they laid my leg to rest. 'Course, I didn't attend the funeral service. I was still in the hospital."

"What kind of mine did you work in?" I asked as I tried to imagine burying my own leg.

He snorted as if I'd asked the dumbest question he'd ever heard. "Carbon City had one of the biggest coal mines in the state. Lots of coal mines around here back in my day. The Northern Pacific built a railroad line up here to haul out the coal. Took out coke, too. There were rows of coke ovens down by the town. Some are still there."

"Coke?" Why would ovens be needed for Coca-Cola? Or did he mean cocaine? Was he a drug addict who imagined he lived long ago?

"Coke. You know, the hard coal that's left after it's heated in the ovens. It's used for fuel."

"Oh."

"For a lad who lives in Carbon City, you don't know much about the place. Ain't you ever gone to see the coke ovens?"

"I don't live here. I've only been here two days. I'm visiting my aunt this summer; she told me about the tree house."

"I used to talk to a girl in this tree house a long time ago. She was a pretty young thing, name of Florence. Her sister came here, too, but the sister couldn't hear me or see me so I only talked to Florence."

"So you're a ghost, not an angel."

"Same thing. *Ghost* sounds frightening, and *angel* sounds comforting. I didn't want to scare you off so I said *angel*. That's one thing book learnin' did for me; I know it's important to use exactly the right word for what you mean."

"Are ghosts and angels really the same? There's no difference?"

"Oh, there's a small difference. Nothing to get worked up about."

"What is it?"

Willie looked annoyed. "If you must know," he said, "a ghost becomes an angel when he's ready to move on. That's when you get the wings and the halo."

"How long have you been a ghost?"

"Since I died. May ninth, nineteen-oh-five. I was thirty-two years old."

"That's more than a hundred years ago! Does it always take so long to move on? When will you become an angel?"

"Drat it, boy, you ask too many questions. I'm not going to be an angel, not now, not ever, because The Boss won't let me."

The Boss? Did he mean God?

Willie scowled and punched one fist into his other palm. "The Boss says I can't get my wings and move on until I get over my anger. He says before I get to be an angel, I must love someone so much that the love fills up my heart and pushes out my resentment."

Willie's scowl deepened. "Ain't nothing going to ease my anger," he said, "and that's a fact. So I'm trapped in limbo. Who would I love? Nobody, that's who. The only ones I loved were my wife and my two boys, and they've already moved on without me."

"You're angry at your wife and sons?"

"Of course not! None of it was their fault. They didn't kill me. We had a good life together, me and Sarah. We had plans for ourselves and for our boys. Big plans! But I didn't get to be part of them. Two years after I died, Sarah married a newspaperman from Tacoma. He raised my boys, not me. He bought my wife a house, not me. She had the daughter she wanted with him, not with me. All because of that Emil Davies." He said the name as if he were spitting out rotten food.

"That's who you're angry at? Emil Davies?"

"His carelessness killed me! He struck a match to light his pipe and *BOOM!* It was the worst explosion the mine ever had. Emil Davies took my life as surely as if he'd held a gun to my head and pulled the trigger. I don't want to see that wicked man ever again, in this life or the next."

"What happened to him? If he was in the mine with you, wasn't he killed, too?"

"He perished and his son with him, and thirteen others besides, including me. The rest are buried in the Carbon City cemetery. All but me. The whole back row of gravestones has the same date of death: May ninth, nineteen-oh-five."

"You weren't buried with your leg?"

Willie shook his head, the angry look still in his eyes. "Sarah told the coroner she didn't think it seemly to dig up the grave where my leg was buried in order to bury the rest of me, but the real reason she didn't plant me there was because she knew I wouldn't want to spend eternity side by side with Emil Davies. Never liked him when he was living and liked him even less after he killed me."

"If the mine blew up and all the miners died, how did Sarah know who caused the explosion?"

"She knew Emil Davies could never wait till he got out of the mine before lighting his dratted corncob pipe. She knew because I complained of it over and over. All of us miners did. We told Emil not to be in such an all-fired hurry for his smoke, but he never listened. When the mine blew, Sarah figured out what had happened. So did everyone else."

"I'm surprised you were still working in the mine with one leg missing."

"I had a peg leg—an uncomfortable chunk of wood that I strapped on every morning."

"Wasn't it hard to walk down into the mine—and back up again?"

"We didn't walk; we rode on hoists. Most days I worked nearly five hundred feet below sea level. The peg leg slowed me down some so I didn't take a rest break with the others. I worked my full shift, then rode the hoist back up. My company brought out ten thousand tons of coal every month."

Willie looked down at his pinned-up pant leg. "Sarah knew how I hated that peg leg so instead of burying it with me, she burned it."

"If you aren't buried with the others who were killed in the explosion, where are you buried?" Even as I asked the question, I realized how bizarre it sounded. Anyone eavesdropping on this conversation would think Willie and I were both crazy.

CHAPTER SEVEN

Willie didn't seem to find our conversation odd. He acted as if we met in the tree house every day for a pleasant chat.

"Sarah buried me by my favorite fishing spot. She got her brothers and mine to help her. They went to where the coroner had all of us dead miners laid out, wrapped in burlap, and when she said she'd come to claim her husband's body, the coroner agreed.

"The brothers put me in a cart behind my horse and led the horse up the hill to a place I always fished, along the Carbon River. They dug the grave deep and buried me there, and Sarah planted wild roses on the spot. She was a good woman, Sarah. A good woman."

I didn't know what to say. More than a century later, I could tell he still yearned for the woman who had been his wife.

"The only thing Sarah didn't do for me," Willie said, "was to remove my leg bones from the cemetery and bury them with the rest of me. I want to be all together in one place, far from Emil Davies."

"Did you tell her what you want? Did you ask her to have the bones dug up and moved?"

A great sadness came into his eyes, and he looked down at his boot. "Sarah couldn't hear me," he said. "I tried and tried to talk to her, but she never heard any of it. She never saw me after I died, never sensed my presence. My boys couldn't see or hear me, either. Most people can't. I move among them, and they don't notice. The girl, Florence, was the first to see and hear me. You're the second."

Florence. I thought about Aunt Ethel's peacock. If anyone could shed some light on that situation, it was Willie. "Do you know what happened to Florence?" I asked.

"It scared her that she could see me when her sister couldn't so she quit coming to the tree house. Sure did miss that girl. It gets lonely with no one to talk to."

"Couldn't you have gone to her house to see her when her sister wasn't there?"

"I could have, but once she got afraid of me, I left her alone. All I wanted was someone to talk to, and you can't hold a conversation when the other person's jumpy as a jackrabbit. I watched her sometimes, though. Saw her grow up, teach school, take care of the critters. I liked that about her—she was kind to the animals."

"What about after she died?"

"She must have moved on right away. Never saw her as a ghost."

"Do people ever come back to Earth as animals or birds?"

"Boy, you don't know much about the hereafter, do you? Why would a person turn into a bird?"

"My Aunt Ethel thinks Florence came back as a peacock."

"My Florence? The girl I knew?"

I nodded. "Florence had said when she died she wanted to come back as a peacock, and a few months after her death, this peacock showed up at her house, and it's been there ever since."

"If that ain't the most fanciful tale I ever heard. Boy, you ought to be writing a book yourself."

"It's true! The peacock hangs around the porch, and Aunt Ethel feeds it cracked corn and calls it Florence. Maybe you could go there and see if the peacock recognizes you."

"No. I'm not talkin' to no peacock."

"Please?" The idea of proving or disproving Aunt Ethel's theory excited me. "All you have to do is go talk to the peacock and see what happens. If it's really Florence, she'll remember you."

"If it's Florence and she sees me, she'll be scared, just like when she was a girl. She'll fly away."

I thought how Aunt Ethel didn't want me to bring Mr. Stray home because she feared he could frighten the peacock, but this was different. This was like a scientific experiment.

"The peacock isn't scared of people," I said, "so if it's afraid of you, that'll mean it really IS Florence."

"Or it would mean the peacock's scared of a ghost. Any ghost."

"Please, Willie? It wouldn't take long."

"No. I don't go around frightening people or birds."

"If the peacock is scared, you can leave before it panics and flies away."

Willie thought a moment. "I don't like to go places that I never went while I was alive," he said, "and I never went to Florence's house, but I'll make you a deal. I'll go there for you if you'll do something for me."

"What?"

"Dig up my leg bones, then bury them where the rest of me is buried."

"I can't do that. There are laws against digging up graves."

"You don't have to announce it to the sheriff. All you have to do is get a shovel, go there alone, and dig."

"What if somebody saw me?"

Oh man, I thought, as I imagined the police calling Mom to say I'd been arrested for grave robbery. My palms started to sweat just thinking about it.

"You can do it at night. Nobody's there at night. Nobody's there in the daytime, either, most of the time. That graveyard is not exactly a lively place." His eyes crinkled at the edges, and I could tell he wanted me to acknowledge his joke.

I shook my head. "No way," I said. "I'm not sneaking into a cemetery at night, or any other time, to dig up one of the graves. It's too risky."

"Will you at least go to the cemetery and find where my leg's buried? You can look around, see how easy it would be, and then decide."

After what Willie had told me, I was curious about the cemetery. I wanted to see the row of gravestones all with the same date of death, and I wondered what it said on his leg's gravestone. HERE LIES THE LEG OF WILLIE MARTIN? Or BELOVED LEG?

"I guess I could look at the grave." I didn't mind agreeing to that. I had no intention of digging anywhere, but there's no law against looking around in a cemetery.

"Good," Willie said. "Let's go." He pointed out the door. "You can walk there on the old railroad bed."

"I can't do it now; I have to get home. Aunt Ethel will worry if I stay away too long. I'll go to the cemetery tomorrow morning."

"After you've been there, I'll show you where the rest of me is buried, so you'll know where to take the leg bones."

"I'm only going to look at the grave, Willie. I'm not going to dig up your leg bones."

"I wonder if the peacock would know me," he said. "I thought you were curious."

"I'm not curious enough to get myself arrested."

We stared at each other for several seconds while his sad eyes pleaded silently.

"You're my only hope," he said. "I wanted to ask Florence to do it, but she got scared and quit coming here before I got up my nerve to ask her."

"It only took you about fifteen minutes to ask me."

"I've been waiting all these years for someone else I could ask, someone who can hear me. That's one reason I started spending time in the library. I thought people who read ghost stories might be able to see me, so I hung around the supernatural section waiting to be noticed, but it never happened."

I envisioned Willie, waiting and hoping for so many years. It made me sad.

"All these years," Willie said, "I've told myself that if I ever meet a living person who can hear and see me, I'll ask for their help right away. I won't take a chance that they'll leave and not return, like Florence did. Now here you are, the only one who can help me. If you won't do it, it might be another fifty years before anyone else sees me."

Ten minutes earlier, when I first saw Willie, I had been scared silly. Now I felt sorry for him.

"I'll think about it," I said.

The ghost smiled at me. "I'll see you in the morning," he said just before he vanished.

I looked out the window but saw only the woods. No old coal miner.

I took a deep breath. I knew why I'd agreed to go to the cemetery. Besides being curious about the graveyard, I *liked* Willie.

In every ghost story I've ever read, the characters are afraid of the ghost—so why was I calmly carrying on a conversation with one?

CHAPTER EIGHT

I climbed down the ladder, then spotted Mr. Stray on the same rock where he'd watched me before. I sat down by his food. Soon he approached, walking slowly as if unsure whether or not he should come close. When I didn't move, he stopped beside me and sniffed my shoe.

"Good kitty," I said.

He leaned against me, rubbing the side of his face against the sole of my shoe. I wanted to pet him, but I was afraid if I reached toward him, he'd run off, so I sat still and continued to talk to him. Soon he stretched forward and sniffed my pant leg.

That's when I realized that Mr. Stray was really Mrs. Stray!

This cat was nursing kittens! No wonder she was so hungry. I wondered where the kittens were.

Hidden in the brush somewhere, I supposed.

My plan to tame the cat and find a home for it had just become more complicated. If Aunt Ethel was unhappy about one stray cat, what would she say about raising kittens?

I made a fist and slowly extended it toward Mrs. Stray. She sniffed my hand thoroughly, but when I tried to touch her, she backed away. She crouched at the water bowl and lapped quickly, her pink tongue darting in and out. Then she moved to the food dish, keeping a wary eye on me.

When she finished drinking and eating, she left.

As I walked back to the house, my brain buzzed with excitement about the ghost and the mother cat, but I decided not to tell Aunt Ethel about either of them. Since Aunt Ethel had not been able to see or hear Willie when she was younger, she might not want me to talk to him, and I didn't want to push my luck about taming the cat. Let her get used to the idea of one cat before I sprang a litter of kittens on her.

The summer that I had thought would be boring was already filled with secrets and excitement.

Aunt Ethel seemed relieved to see me. "I was afraid you got lost," she said.

"I'm sorry if I worried you. I was in the tree

house, reading." And talking to a ghost and feeding Mrs. Stray.

She smiled. "You sound like Florence. She always had her nose in a book and forgot the time. Get washed up; our dinner's almost ready."

"It smells great," I said as I washed my hands at the kitchen sink.

"Cheese omelets and sliced tomatoes. Another favorite dinner. Fried potatoes, too, and cantaloupe. It's good to have someone to cook for again. I've always liked to cook, but Florence didn't, so we agreed I'd be the cook and she'd be the one to clean up."

Taking the hint, I said, "I'll do the dishes. That can be my job all summer."

As we ate, I asked, "Do you have any books about Carbon City history? I'd like to learn about the coal mines."

"There might be some in Florence's room. I never got around to sorting through her things."

"Is it OK if I look?" I already knew which room she meant, because she had called it "my sister's room" that first night when she showed me around the house.

"Read anything you want," she said. "Nothing made Florence happier than a youngster who liked to read. If you don't find anything you like, we can stop at the library the next time we drive to Diamond Hill for groceries."

After dinner and two pieces of the best chocolate cake I'd ever eaten, I washed the dishes, then found two apple crates in Florence's room. Stacked on their sides to make shelves, they were filled with old books.

Several were books for children: *The Five Little Peppers and How They Grew*, *The Adventures of Sammy Jay*, and *The Birds' Christmas Carol*. All had names written inside the cover, but none of the names was Florence. She must have bought used books, or maybe they were donated to the school by the parents of her pupils. Compared to the mystery and adventure books I had brought with me, these didn't look very exciting.

In the second apple crate, I found two slim volumes—pamphlets, really—on the history of Carbon City. One, called "Mining Disasters," consisted of reprints of old newspaper articles about the area. I began to read, skimming until I saw the date, May 10, 1905.

EXPLOSION IN CARBON CITY MINE
FIFTEEN MEN MEET THEIR DEATH
Widowed women and fatherless children wept near the mouth of Mine Number Five's tunnel yes-

terday, as the bodies of fifteen miners were hauled up out of the mine on the long incline tramway.

An explosion occurred shortly after noon on May 9. Mine Superintendent Richard Jones speculated that carelessness and disobedience of orders by one or more of the miners caused the tragedy. "Someone must have struck a match or exposed the flame of his safety light," the superintendent said, "probably to light his pipe."

Details of the disaster are still meager.

The article ended with the names of the dead, including Emil Davies and Wilber Martin. I stared at Willie's name. I had talked to him that very afternoon, yet here was proof he had died more than a century ago, and his death took place exactly where and when he had described it.

Why could I see a ghost when others couldn't? Did I have special psychic powers? Mom sometimes watched a TV show where a man helped people talk to their dead relatives. I liked to watch the show with her, but it gave me the creeps to think I might have such ability.

If I could see one ghost, maybe I'd see more of them, and what better place for them to show up than a graveyard? What if all of the dead miners decided to pay me a visit? I regretted my promise to go to the cemetery the next morning.

I put the two pamphlets in my own room. Then I went down to talk to Aunt Ethel.

"Why did Aunt Florence think the tree house was haunted?" I asked, hoping I sounded casual and not overly curious.

Aunt Ethel put down the book she was reading. "Florence claimed a ghost visited us whenever we were in the tree house—a coal miner who had died in one of the explosions. I never saw him, but Florence swore up and down he'd come inside the tree house and talk to her. She even described his clothes, and she said he smelled of coal dust. At first I thought she made it up to annoy me because I didn't see him, but when she got frightened, I knew she wasn't pretending."

"Why was she scared of him?"

"She wasn't at first. She liked seeing him when I couldn't. It made her feel special. Later it bothered her that he always came when we were there. She feared he might start popping up other places, and she wouldn't be able to get rid of him. So she quit going to the tree house."

"Did she know his name?"

"If she did, I don't remember it. I do remember he had only one leg, which seemed odd." She put a bookmark in her page and looked directly at me. "Why are you so interested in Florence's old ghost? You didn't see anything like that today, did you?"

Who, me?

I shrugged. "I'm curious. I like ghost stories." My reply wasn't the truth, the whole truth, and nothing but the truth, but it wasn't a lie, either.

"Did you find any history books in Florence's room?" Aunt Ethel asked.

"A couple. I'd like to visit the coke ovens sometime."

"They're overgrown and crumbling now, but you can still find them. When we go to town for the mail next week, I'll show you where they are."

"You only pick up mail once a week?"

"No need to go more often. It's mostly ads and bills."

"Maybe I'll hear from my parents." Since Aunt Ethel did not have e-mail, Mom had made arrangements with Mrs. Arbuckle, Steven's office manager in Minneapolis, to forward letters between India and Carbon City. When I wrote to Mom and Steven, I was supposed to mail the letters to Mrs. Arbuckle, who would scan them and e-mail them to Mom and Steven. They would e-mail to Mrs. Arbuckle all their letters to me, which she would print and send to Aunt Ethel's post office box.

Aunt Ethel shifted in her recliner and looked closely at me. "Do you miss your folks?"

I didn't answer right away. I still felt angry at Mom and Steven for shipping me off for the summer, but I missed them, too.

Seeing my hesitation, Aunt Ethel stood up. "I have the perfect cure for being lonely," she said. "Rocky road ice cream."

"Can I have mine with another piece of that chocolate cake?"

She beamed at me. "You like your Welcome cake?"

"It's the best cake I ever ate."

"Good cake is one of life's great joys," she said. "Cake making is an art, you know. You can't dump a mix out of a box and expect to create a delicate cake that melts on the tongue. It takes practice—and sour cream."

"You can practice as much as you want while I'm here," I said.

"I'm glad you came," Aunt Ethel said. "I hadn't realized how much I missed having someone else in the house. Muriel comes two or three times a week, but she never stays overnight. It's good to have a companion."

As we ate, I said, "I read about the Carbon City cemetery in one of Aunt Florence's books. I might go there tomorrow to look around."

"It isn't far. You can walk there."

I nearly said *I know; the ghost told me,* but caught myself before the words came out. "It's the cemetery we passed on our way home from Carbon City, isn't it?"

"Yes. The road goes past it, but from here it's safer to walk on the old railroad bed. The rails were torn up years ago, but the ground they were on is hard. It's used as a trail by hikers and horsemen. Follow the trail and go right at the Y; you'll end up in the cemetery. Florence is buried there."

Yikes. Maybe going to the cemetery wasn't such a great idea. I wasn't sure I could handle Willie's leg AND Aunt Florence.

Aunt Ethel went to bed as soon as she finished her ice cream.

I sat in bed reading old newspaper accounts of the coal mines until I fell asleep.

After I did the breakfast dishes the next morning, I went to the tree house. Mrs. Stray, or some other animal, had eaten the cat food so I refilled the bowl, but I didn't see the cat. I didn't see the ghost, either.

I headed the direction Willie had pointed the day before, looking for the old railroad bed. Every so often I saw deer droppings, but I didn't see any animals.

I had hiked about ten minutes when I spotted a trail. I consulted my compass, then turned south on the trail. A weathered wooden pole stood at the side of the trail, with a cross pole about seven feet up. The old newspaper stories told about telegraphs sent after the mine explosions; this must be the remnant of a telegraph pole.

I'd gone about half a mile when I spotted a piece of rusty metal sticking up out of the dirt. I dug around it with my fingers, then pried up an old railroad spike. The spike was six inches long and looked like an overgrown nail, except the shaft was square instead of round with a flattened end, much like a chisel. I knew it would have been used to nail down the old railroad tracks for the train cars that hauled the coal. I stuck the spike in my pocket and walked on, feeling as if I were hiking backward into history.

From then on, I kept my head down as I walked. Maybe I'd find more old railroad spikes or even a piece of rail.

A mile or so after I found the spike, the path split. One part went straight; the other veered to the right, up an incline. I turned right and soon looked down on an old cemetery.

Once-white gravestones were dark gray; some had

toppled to the ground. There were a few large markers, but most were about two feet high—flat slabs with rounded tops.

I went to the back row where fourteen identical grave markers stood side by side, sticking up like concrete headboards. I read the names, including Emil Davies, and saw they all had the same date of death: May 9, 1905. All of the miners from that explosion were buried there except Willie.

Some fast subtraction from the dates of birth told me most of the men had lived less than thirty years. Emil Davies, at thirty-seven, was the oldest. His son, Victor, age sixteen, was the youngest.

Sadness for these lost lives brought a lump to my throat. The newspaper account I'd read last night had seemed far removed, a tragedy in a past century that had nothing to do with me. Seeing these names and dates made the disastrous explosion vividly real in my mind.

I turned away from the last row and surveyed my surroundings. Faded plastic flowers and a few small American flags—probably left from Memorial Day—decorated half a dozen graves. The rest were unadorned.

No one else was visiting a grave, no joggers ran

past, and no cars drove by on the road that bordered the far side of the cemetery. Willie was right; I could dig here unobserved if I wanted to.

Did I?

Back home, I would not have considered such an action for one second, knowing the trouble I'd be in if I got caught. Why should it be different here?

Although I was still angry at Mom for going to India and sending me here for the summer, I wasn't so mad that I wanted to get myself hauled off to juvenile detention.

Still, now that I'd seen the cemetery, the idea of helping the ghost appealed to me. It was Willie's leg, and he wanted it moved. Shouldn't this be his decision?

There are laws against digging up graves because grave robbers steal jewelry or other valuables that were buried with the body. I only wanted to find Willie's leg bones so I could grant his wish to have his leg buried with the rest of his body.

A voice in my head whispered, *Tell that to the police if someone sees you.*

Since other people couldn't see or hear Willie, there would be no way to prove my story if I got caught.

CHAPTER NINE

I walked up and down the rows of graves, arguing with myself as I searched for the spot where Willie's leg was buried.

I didn't find it. I did find Florence's grave, though.

FLORENCE HODGE
BELOVED DAUGHTER, SISTER, AND TEACHER

"Ethel misses you, Florence," I whispered, "and Steven remembers you fondly." I thought, so does Willie, but I decided not to mention him.

Of course, I didn't believe Florence could hear me, no matter what I said to her. If Aunt Ethel was right, Florence was now perched on the porch rail. If Willie was right, Florence had moved on and was an angel by now. Either way, she wasn't lying under the sod, listening to me. Still, it seemed natural to talk to her.

I retraced my steps, reading each marker carefully, still searching for Willie's leg. I was about to give up when Willie appeared beside me.

"There it is," he said, pointing at a flat marker about four by eight inches big that I hadn't noticed at the edge of the graveyard.

"It's about time you showed up," I said.

I knelt beside the marker he pointed to. It was far smaller than the others, and grass had encroached along the edges, giving it an uneven look. I bent to brush a fallen leaf from the marker and saw W.M.M. etched on the top.

"No wonder I missed it," I said. "I was looking for your name or the nineteen-oh-three date."

"Didn't want my whole name put on. Only my initials."

"What's your middle name?"

"Michael."

"That's my middle name!"

We smiled at each other.

"Will you do it?" he asked.

"I don't know, Willie. I could get in big-time trouble if I'm caught."

Visions of being grounded for a year floated

through my mind. On the other hand, I had no friends in Minneapolis yet, so what did it matter if Mom and Steven took away phone privileges and made me stay home all the time?

I considered discussing the situation with Aunt Ethel—but she hadn't been able to see Willie when Florence did and had never believed the tree house was haunted, so she probably wouldn't believe that I saw him now. Or, if she did, she'd make me stay away from it.

Most actions that are against the law are obviously wrong—things like shoplifting or arson—and I'd never, ever do them. This was different. Digging up Willie's leg was probably illegal, but I didn't think it was immoral. I thought it was the right thing to do.

"I'll be your lookout," Willie said. "I can warn you if anyone's coming."

"I hope I won't regret this."

"You'll do it?"

"I'll do it."

A grin spread across Willie's face, making him look lit up from the inside. "Go get a spade. You can dig right now."

"Not so fast. Before I dig up your leg, I need to know where I'm going to take it. Once I have it, I'll want to get it buried again as quickly as I can."

"Follow me. I'll show you where I'm buried."

Oh, man. It's so bizarre when he says stuff like that. I hoped I wasn't making a huge mistake.

"How far is it from here?" I asked. I was already a long way from Aunt Ethel's house, and my legs were still sore from the bike ride to Carbon City plus all the hiking I'd done.

"It's two or three miles up the hill. There's a gravel road that fishermen use."

I considered.

"It's all downhill going home," Willie said. "I went there yesterday after you left, so I know I can find the place."

Despite my aching legs, I decided it was better to go now than to put it off another day. I followed Willie out of the cemetery.

He led me up the road toward Aunt Ethel's house. She needn't have worried about safety; no cars came along. We continued past her driveway, where the road narrowed. It soon became a gravel road impassable by anything other than an off-road vehicle. The average school desk would have fit in some of the potholes. I picked my way around them, hoping I didn't slip and fall. If I injured myself here, I wouldn't be found for months.

Having only one leg didn't hinder Willie at all.

While I stumbled up the rutted road, he glided over the surface without ever touching it. Twice he disappeared. He was like a patch of fog, here one minute and gone the next.

Once when he was visible, I said, "I'm not sure I'll be able to do this. I had hoped I could ride a bike to the cemetery. After I dug up your leg casket, I planned to tie it to the bike, then ride the bike to where the rest of you is buried. Forget that plan. I'll never be able to ride a bike up this road. It'll be a tough walk carrying a shovel and a small casket."

"You can leave the casket. Just bring the bones."

"No way. I'm not opening up that coffin and taking the bones out."

Willie snorted, as if to say, *Huh! What a wimp.* "They're only bones. They won't bite you."

"I can still change my mind, you know." I kicked a small stone to one side. "I don't have to do this."

He stopped gliding. His expression looked the way I'd felt when I heard Mom say I couldn't be on the summer baseball team. "You promised," he said. "You told me you'd help me."

"Oh, all right, I won't back out, but let me do it my way. The leg stays in the casket."

"The rest of me isn't in a box. I want everything together."

I glared at him. "You are the most demanding ghost I've ever known."

His eyes crinkled at the edges. "I'm also the nicest ghost you've ever known. Friendly. Talkative. Willing to share information. I'd give you the shirt off my back, only you probably don't want it."

Looking at his coal-smudged shirt, I couldn't help laughing.

"You could bring the casket up here," Willie suggested, "then open it and dump the leg bones in with the rest of me. You wouldn't have to touch them."

"What'll I do with the casket?"

"Throw it away. Keep it as a souvenir. Take it back to the cemetery and rebury it. Who cares? It's only an old wooden box."

Before I could respond, he vanished again.

"I wish you wouldn't do that," I muttered.

I sat on a boulder to catch my breath and rest my own legs, which felt as if they would fall off any second. I wished I'd brought drinking water.

I thought about Willie's casket. If it was wooden, as he said, it might be rotted by now. I might have no choice but to pluck the bones from the dirt.

I wondered how many bones there were. Willie's knee, leg, ankle, foot, toes—would they all still be connected?

Grossed out by my imagination, I stood and plodded on up the hill. There were fewer trees now and more rocks. I heard water rushing ahead of me; the river wasn't far.

The trees ended, replaced by rocks and sand, which led to the river. It gurgled over the rocks, shallow at the edges.

As soon as I saw it, I removed my shoes and socks, rolled up my jeans, and waded in. I splashed some of the cold water on my face and rubbed it on my arms.

It was too cold to stay in long. I sat on the rocky beach, letting the sun dry my feet.

"This is where I used to fish."

I no longer jumped when Willie reappeared, which shows you can get used to most anything.

"Caught many a trout in this river. There's nothing like fresh trout, panfried over a fire." He sighed and sat beside me. "I miss eating," he said. "When you're alive, you don't give it a second thought. Oh, you might wonder what's for dinner or look forward to a favorite meal now and then, but you don't appreciate being able to put a fork in your mouth and actually taste the food. I miss Sarah's bread the most. That woman baked the best bread—crunchy on the outside, soft on the inside."

"Sometimes my mom bakes cinnamon rolls. The

whole house smells good while they're in the oven."
Suddenly, I yearned for home. I longed to sit at the
kitchen table with Mom and Steven, all of us eating
cinnamon rolls before they cooled, joking about what
pigs we were.

I wondered if Mom and Steven were safe in India.
Did Mom enjoy the job? What was New Delhi like?
Was the food good?

"There's my grave," Willie said. "Right where the
river bends."

I put on my shoes and socks, then followed him
to a patch of ground about thirty feet from the river's
edge, where a tangle of pricker bushes sent thorny
branches crawling over the rocks.

"Are you sure?"

"Sarah planted a rosebush there. It blossomed the
first few years; then it got scrawny and went wild.
Now it looks dead from lack of water."

Some of the branches were more than an inch
thick and covered with thorns the size of Mrs. Stray's
toenails. I wondered if there might be a small saw in
Aunt Ethel's barn.

I'll need to wear long sleeves, I thought, and
gloves. Gloves seemed a good idea, anyway, especially
if the wooden box had rotted.

"Let's go," Willie said. "We have work to do."

"I'm not coming back today," I said. "It's too far."

"It's only a few miles."

"Easy for you to say. I'm the one climbing up and down hills. All you do is float."

"It won't take long. You can get the tools you need, dig up my leg, bring it here, bury it, and be home in time for supper."

"No. If I tried to do all of that today, we'd both be dead."

"Tomorrow, then?"

"If I can still move tomorrow, which I seriously doubt, I'll do it early in the morning."

"I've already waited more than a hundred years," Willie said. "It won't kill me to wait one more day."

I groaned at his joke.

"Thank you," Willie said. "Thank you for helping me."

CHAPTER TEN

Willie talked nonstop on our way downhill. I think he was afraid if he let me say anything, I might change my mind about moving his leg bones.

"When I was alive," he said, "the mines employed a thousand men. A lumber mill and a stone quarry thrived in Carbon City, too. Those coke ovens looked like big ol' beehives. They blazed away night and day."

It was hard for me to picture so much activity in sleepy little Carbon City.

Willie went with me as far as Aunt Ethel's driveway; then I walked alone back to the house.

As I hung the compass on the nail, I was surprised to hear the mantel clock strike twice. I felt as if I'd been gone all day, but it was only two o'clock.

Willie was right. I probably could have dug the bones and reburied them yet today.

My tired legs were not the whole reason I had refused. I needed time to think through the whole process, to make sure I wasn't overlooking a potential problem. Once I started digging, I wanted to finish the whole plan quickly.

A note from Aunt Ethel was taped to the door.

Josh:
   Muriel invited me to go to the raspberry
farm with her to get fresh berries.
                                    Aunt Ethel

After eating a peanut butter sandwich, an apple, and a piece of chocolate cake, I went to the barn and found a sturdy spade and a small hatchet for hacking through the rosebush. The hatchet fit in my backpack, but I'd have to carry the spade.

I decided to leave the casket behind, rotted or not, and put the bones in my backpack. The less weight I had to haul uphill, the better.

Holding the spade handle in my hands, I tried to imagine actually digging in the cemetery. Thinking about it made my palms sweaty. I wasn't afraid of seeing the bones, but I was definitely scared of getting caught. No matter how much I justified moving Willie's leg, I couldn't ignore the fact that if anyone saw me, I would have a huge problem.

Maybe I should dig the leg up at night, as Willie had suggested. But at night I'd have to use a flashlight to see what I was doing, and that might call more attention to me than if I did it in the daytime.

In my mind, I returned to the cemetery, thinking how it would look after dark. I remembered the road that went past it. I saw the rows of gravestones and the faded flowers.

Flowers! That's what I needed! I would take flowers with me so if someone happened to pass by and see me digging, I would appear to be planting flowers on a grave. After I had the leg bones safely in my backpack, I would put the flowers in the hole so it wouldn't be obvious that the grave had been disturbed and something removed.

Next problem: Where was I going to get flowers to plant on the grave? Back home, every large grocery store had a floral department that sold flowering plants; but the Carbon City Market didn't sell flowers, and there were no other retail stores within bike-riding distance. I couldn't ask Aunt Ethel to drive me to Diamond Hill to buy flowers unless I told her why I wanted them, and that was out of the question.

Then I remembered the flowers along the sides of the house. I could dig up a clump of those yellow daisies, keep them in a bucket of water overnight, and plant them in the cemetery tomorrow morning.

I decided to dig two clumps of daisies and plant one on Aunt Florence's grave. That way I wouldn't feel so guilty about taking Aunt Ethel's flowers without permission.

I wondered when Aunt Ethel would get home. Her note didn't say what time she'd left, but this was probably my best chance to dig up flowers. Hoping I'd hear Muriel's car when it came down the driveway, I got the shovel and dug up enough daisies to fill a big bucket. I took small clumps from several spots so it wouldn't be obvious that flowers were missing.

I carried the daisies and the shovel out to the tree house and looked around for Mrs. Stray. If I expected to tame her and her babies, I needed to spend as much time with her as I could, but I didn't see her. The food hadn't been touched since I had refilled the bowl that morning. I hoped Mrs. Stray was okay.

I was eager to tell Willie my brilliant idea about

the daisies, but he didn't show up, so I climbed the ladder and went inside.

I was too nervous to read. All I could think about was what I planned to do the next day. I looked out the tree-house window at the cat dishes below.

A twig snapped. Three deer stood near the base of the tree house, their black tails flicking as they grazed. I scarcely breathed, for fear I would startle them. The largest deer kept looking back into the woods as if she saw or heard something. Soon the other two stopped eating and looked in the same direction. Their ears perked forward; all of them seemed curious.

The big doe took two steps toward whatever she was watching, then stopped again. A few seconds later, I spotted Mrs. Stray moving slowly toward her bowls. The deers' eyes followed her.

She walked a few feet, then stopped and looked at the deer before continuing. When she reached the bowls and started lapping the water, the three inquisitive deer stepped closer. I imagined them saying, *What in the world is that animal? Let's go closer and find out what it smells like.*

Mrs. Stray crunched some cat food, but she kept glancing up nervously as the deer approached. When they were only three feet away, she fled into the woods. The deer trotted after her.

I realized I was smiling. I'd climbed the ladder feeling anxious, but the animals and the forest made me happy.

If I had any sense, I thought, I'd leave well enough alone—enjoy the woods, try to tame the cats, and not take a chance of possibly ruining my summer by getting arrested for removing bones from the cemetery.

Even as I thought that, I knew I would follow my plan to help Willie. If I didn't help him, who would? Willie needed a friend and, as far as I knew, there were no other candidates.

I returned to Aunt Ethel's house. She was in the kitchen, rinsing a colander full of raspberries. "Look what we're having for dinner," she said.

I helped myself to a raspberry. "Yum," I said. I took another berry.

"I stopped at the post office on the way home. There weren't any letters."

I knew it was too soon to get a letter from Mom, but I couldn't help feeling disappointed.

My plans for the next day soon took over my thoughts. I needed to have everything ready so I could get an early start.

"Is there any bottled water?" I asked. "I get thirsty in the tree house."

Aunt Ethel said, "No point paying for bottled water when perfectly good well water runs out of the faucet free." She opened a cupboard and handed me an empty plastic container.

"You can use this."

I filled the container with water, pushed the lid on tight, and put it in my backpack, hoping it wouldn't leak.

I added a brown bathroom towel to my backpack, to wrap the leg bones in. I looked under the bathroom sink, hoping to find a pair of rubber gloves to borrow, but there weren't any. I hadn't found any garden gloves in the barn, either. I decided not to ask Aunt Ethel for gloves because I didn't want to explain why I needed them, and I couldn't think of a believable excuse. The less I said about my intentions, the fewer questions she would have. If the rose thorns were too bad, I'd pull my shirtsleeves down over my hands.

I considered packing myself a lunch but decided against it. Once I started this project, I wanted to finish as quickly as I could, and I already had enough to carry. Besides, I wouldn't want to eat a sandwich that had shared the backpack with Willie's leg bones.

Before I went to bed, I wrote another letter:

June 18

Dear Mom and Steven,

    I found the tree house, and it's haunted!
A ghost named Willie, an old coal miner, hangs
out there. Aunt Ethel says Aunt Florence
used to see him, and now I see him.

    Willie wants me to dig up his leg bones,
which are buried in the Carbon City ceme-
tery, and move them to where the rest of his
body is buried.

    I'm going to do it.

Your grave-digger son,

Josh

I put down my pen, smiling to myself as I imagined how Mom and Steven would react when they read this. I had not yet mailed the first two letters; I hadn't known Aunt Ethel was going to the post office today.

Now I debated whether to send the letters one at a time or all together. I decided one at a time would probably be best, so I put the first letter, about shooting the bat, in one of the addressed, stamped envelopes Mom had sent with me.

"You'll have no excuse not to write," she had said when she gave me the envelopes.

I laid the sealed envelope and the other two letters in the drawer with my underwear.

Next I wrote a note to Aunt Ethel.

I've gone to visit the cemetery again. Then I plan to hike up an old gravel road to the Carbon River. I might not get home until late, so don't worry if I miss lunch.

I planned to leave Aunt Ethel's note on my bed when I left in the morning. In case I didn't return, I wanted the Search and Rescue teams to know where to look for me.

The next day was Friday, June 19, the day the summer team played its first tournament game. I wondered what the other guys on the team would think if they knew what I was doing while they played baseball. They'd never believe it.

I knew tomorrow was either going to be the most exciting day of my life or the most disastrous.

CHAPTER ELEVEN

Mr. Turlep did not look like a criminal. Wearing a navy blue suit, white shirt, and a tan striped necktie, he watched as his assistant locked the bank's front door. He waited while his employees left their posts, said good night to each other, and headed home.

When he was the only one left in the building, he took the calendar out of his top desk drawer and, as he did each day at closing time, drew a big black *X* through June 18, that day's date. He'd done this every day for more than two years, even taking the calendar home with him on weekends so he could *X* out the Saturdays and Sundays. Except on the thirteenth of each month. Mr. Turlep felt it might be bad luck to cross out the number thirteen, so every month he left it untouched.

Each *X* brought him one day closer to the happiest moment of his life: the time when he would walk out of the Hillside Bank forever, retrieve the money, and start his new life in Florida. He would spend every day fishing in the sunshine and would never again—not once—sit behind a desk in a bank.

Mr. Turlep had begun working at the bank forty-three years ago as a trainee and had slowly worked his way up to manager. He had relished the work for many years, but he didn't enjoy it anymore. Now the government regulations and the unnecessary paperwork and the intense competition with huge national banks had taken all the pleasure away. Even the customers were less polite and more demanding. Everyone wanted to borrow money, but no one wanted to save it.

Mr. Turlep loosened his necktie and went out the back entrance, making sure the door locked securely behind him. He walked to his car, started the engine, and began the second part of his biweekly ritual.

Twice a week on his way home from work, he drove thirty miles out of his way in order to go past the sleepy little Carbon City cemetery, where he'd buried the money. He didn't worry that someone might accidentally find it; in all the months (seven hundred eighty days, to be exact) since he'd hidden it, he had never seen a person in the cemetery.

His visits were a way to comfort himself after a hard day's work and to stay focused on his plan of never having to work again. He liked to drive slowly past the little graveyard, his eyes on the spot he'd chosen, while he thought of what lay hidden there and how it would soon enrich his life.

By now, he'd nearly forgotten that the money didn't really belong to him, that he'd taken it at gunpoint from two terrified bank customers as they approached the night-deposit box. He had erased from his memory the fact that the entire community had been outraged by the theft of the Cash for Critters proceeds.

At the time, he had pretended to be as furious as everyone else. As manager of the Hillside Bank, he had posted a one-thousand-dollar reward for information leading to the arrest of the thief, and then he had personally matched that amount.

When his customers thanked him for his generosity, he had said, "Whoever did this robbed us not only of our animal shelter, but also of our community spirit. It's tragic, that's what it is. Tragic!"

Much of the money was in one-hundred-dollar bills. The rest he exchanged over a week's time for more one-hundred-dollar bills until that was all he had. He bundled the bills securely, locked them in the small metal box he'd bought, and then used the ideal hiding place.

The crime was never solved, so eventually people quit talking about it and went about their business. The police had meth labs, drunk drivers, and assaults to deal with each day. With no clues to go on and no suspect, the theft of the Cash for Critters money slid gradually into the "unsolved" category, where the case was ignored.

The money was not forgotten by Mr. Turlep. Each day at closing time, as he Xed out the date, he thought of the difference the box of cash would make in his life. Without it, his retirement years would be meager. With it, he could live out his dream.

He should not have had to resort to theft in order to have a comfortable retirement. After years of living frugally and saving his money, Mr. Turlep's dreams had been crushed by a corporate scandal that cost him, through no fault of his own, all his savings. Unscrupulous officers of the company where Mr. Turlep's pension was invested had bilked the shareholders of millions. The money he had counted on for his retirement vanished.

When the news sank in that he had lost his personal savings and his bank pension, which were invested in the same place, Mr. Turlep changed. Overnight the man who had always been a mild-mannered, law-abiding banker became a bitter, cold-hearted criminal.

He knew his Social Security income wouldn't buy the coveted condo on the beach, nor would it be enough to pay for weekly deep-sea fishing trips. The life he'd dreamed of for years had been within his grasp, and then it had vanished—until he'd planned and pulled off the perfect crime.

Who had been hurt by his theft? Nobody. It wasn't as if he'd taken food from starving children or medicines from cancer patients. Oh, sure, a few hundred dogs and cats were left to fend for themselves each year instead of getting food, veterinary care, and loving homes. No big deal about that. They weren't any worse off than they'd always been around here.

Mr. Turlep had worked hard all his life; he deserved a happy retirement. Now, with only one more day to go, the time was almost here. Tomorrow—Friday, June 19—he would make the last X, leave the bank for the last time, and make his final drive to the Carbon City cemetery.

Tonight he would finish packing. Tomorrow he would dig up his money and head for Florida. Those fish were waiting for him.

CHAPTER TWELVE

Florence's screaming woke me at sunrise. Instead of pulling the blankets over my head and blocking my ears, I got up, dressed quickly, and propped the note on my pillow.

I planned to grab an apple to eat along the way and tiptoe out of the house without waking Aunt Ethel, but when I got downstairs, she stood in the kitchen with mixing bowls and measuring cups lined up on the counter.

"You're up early," she said.

"So are you."

"I have a cake customer today. She requested carrot cake, and I want to get the carrots grated and the baking done while the kitchen's still cool."

I took an apple from the refrigerator.

"I've been thinking about that stray cat," she said,

"and I decided you were right. You should feed it and tame it and take it to the vet to be neutered. That's what Florence would have done. Then we can try to find someone who will give it a good home."

"Thanks," I said. "She really seems hungry." I decided not to mention any kittens quite yet.

"If you keep the food out by the tree house, the cat probably won't bother Florence."

"OK. That's what I'll do."

"I can drive you to Carbon City to get some cat food this afternoon after I finish my cake."

I couldn't tell her it wasn't necessary because I had already bought cat food. At the rate Mrs. Stray was gobbling the food, I'd need more soon, anyway. I could send my first letter and see if there was any mail for me today. Now that my summer was so exciting, I wasn't as mad at Mom and Steven for sending me here. I wanted to hear from them, to know how they were doing.

I knew they were eager to hear from me, too. I thought about the letters I'd written about the bat, the peacock, and the ghost. Would Mom and Steven worry too much when they read those reports? Maybe I should add a few lines about Mrs. Stray and the chocolate cake, just to let them know I was really OK.

"I'm hiking up the river this morning," I said. "I might not be back until after lunch."

"No hurry. We'll go to Carbon City when you return." She started scrubbing carrots with a brush, then stopped, leaning against the sink.

"Is something wrong?"

"I think I'd better sit for a minute. I feel a bit dizzy."

I took her arm and helped her to a chair.

"My energy gives out now and then," she said. "Inside, I still feel like a schoolgirl, but sometimes my body can't keep up with what I want to do. When that happens, I have to rest a bit."

Although I wanted to get on with my plan, I didn't want to leave if she needed help.

"I'll scrub the carrots," I said. I picked up the brush and turned on the faucet.

When I finished, Aunt Ethel said, "Could you shred them for me, too? I'm feeling better, but I don't have the strength I used to have."

Using her old-fashioned grater, I shredded all the carrots, managing to nick my knuckle once.

Aunt Ethel stood and began sifting flour. "I'm fine now," she said. "You go ahead on your hike."

I watched her measure and stir ingredients for a few minutes, to be sure she didn't have another dizzy spell. Then I slipped on my backpack and headed for the tree house.

Birds chittered in the treetops, greeting the sunshine. I walked quickly.

As I approached the tree house, I saw Mrs. Stray eating breakfast. I stopped moving and watched. I could tell she saw me, but she continued to eat.

"Hello, kitty," I said. "Good kitty, kitty. Nice Mrs. Stray."

Her tail swished back and forth, but she kept eating. A sudden movement in the bushes behind her caught my eye. A small orange kitten trotted out of the undergrowth, followed by a black-and-white kitten. Last came a third kitten, who looked exactly like Mrs. Stray. The kittens nudged their faces under her belly and began to nurse.

I waited, wondering if there were more, but the kitten parade ended. How was I going to tame and rescue four cats? One had been enough of a challenge.

"You going to stand there watching them cats all morning?"

Willie leaned out one of the tree-house windows. The cats scattered when he spoke, so I knew they could hear him. I wondered why animals could hear him when most humans couldn't.

"Hi, Willie."

"I saw your spade and the flowers. Good idea, bringing the flowers."

I picked up the bucket of daisies and the spade, then headed toward the old railroad trail. Willie floated along beside me.

"I'm sorry I can't help you carry those," he said. "'Course, if I could manage a shovel, I'd have dug the leg up myself long ago and wouldn't be bothering you about it."

"I don't mind," I said.

"I look able-bodied, but the truth is, it's all I can do to pick up a book, and I had to practice two years before I could manage that. At first my hands went right through the pages. I've got the hang of it now, and I can move an object or two before I run out of strength."

I didn't answer; I was too jittery for conversation. The closer we got to the cemetery, the more I worried someone would see me and call the police.

I spotted another railroad spike, which I worked loose and put in my backpack.

We reached the Y and turned toward the cemetery.

Soon I stood at the edge of the graveyard, looking carefully in all directions. It was as empty and still as it had been the day before. No cars on the street, no people anywhere in sight. Even the birds were silent.

I planted Florence's flowers first. I walked straight to her grave, then stomped on the shovel. I worked quickly, removing a twelve-inch circle of sod, then digging up the soil inside the circle. I dug down about four inches, then stuck a clump of daisies in the hole. Kneeling beside them, I patted the loose dirt around the roots. I stood, then poured some of the water from the bucket into the indentation around the daisies.

So far, so good.

My heart started to race as I went toward the grave of Willie's leg. My stomach did handsprings, threatening to give back the apple.

When I reached the small w.m.m. stone, I hesitated, looking around and listening for any approaching vehicles. I saw no cars and no people. Except for a fly buzzing around my head, I heard nothing.

I had assumed Willie would want to watch, but he had disappeared. I hoped he was keeping his promise to act as my lookout on the street, ready to alert me if anyone came this way.

I removed the brown towel from my backpack and spread it on the grass beside the grave.

I licked my lips, took a deep breath, and plunged the spade into the dirt. I removed a bigger circle of sod this time, but when I tried to dig deeper into the soil, the tip of the shovel clunked against something hard. A rock? I moved the shovel over a couple of inches and tried again. *Clunk!*

I jabbed the spade into the dirt several times, moving it an inch or two each time, but the result was always the same. *Clunk. Clunk.* It was a metallic sound. Willie had told me his leg's little casket was made of wood, not metal, and surely it would have been buried deeper than this. Each time I tried to dig, my shovel stopped when it was only four or five inches below the surface. If I was hitting a rock, it was a big one, more than a foot across.

I continued to poke the spade into the dirt, moving it farther from the center of the circle, until it went straight down without clunking.

I angled the shovel to take out shallow scoops of dirt. It took only a few minutes of digging to uncover a smooth gray metal surface about eighteen inches long and six inches wide, topped with a handle.

The metal box did not look old. It was enclosed in a heavy plastic bag that had been stapled shut. I didn't know when plastic bags or staplers were invented, but I was fairly certain it was later than 1903. I realized someone else had dug here after Willie's leg was buried and had left this box in the grave.

"Willie?" I said. "Are you here?"

No answer.

I pulled apart the bag where it was stapled and opened the plastic so I could grip the box's handle. I yanked as hard as I could, but the box stayed securely in the ground.

Abandoning the spade and digging with my fingers, I loosened the dirt around the metal until I could lift the box out of the hole. I tore away the rest of the plastic bag. The gray metal box looked like the small fireproof box that Gramma kept the deed to her house and other important papers in. A brass lock held the top closed. I wondered who had the key.

The box fit in my backpack so I stuffed it in and continued to dig. About two feet farther down, I came to chunks of rotted wood. Kneeling in the dirt on the side of the grave, I picked the pieces of wood out of the hole and tossed them aside.

The hole smelled like rich garden soil after a rain. I hoped there were no worms. I've never minded handling worms when I go fishing, but this was different.

Gritting my teeth, I thrust both hands into the damp dirt at the bottom of the hole.

My fingers closed on something solid. I swallowed hard, then pulled it up. I tried to remember the names of human leg bones. Tibia? Femur? Which was the big one?

All I knew for sure was that I held part of Willie's leg in my hand. I didn't bother to brush off the dirt that clung to the large bone. I laid the bone on the towel and stuck my hands back in the hole.

Nervous sweat soaked my shirt. If anyone had sneaked up behind me and whispered, "Boo," I would have fainted and toppled headfirst into the open grave.

CHAPTER THIRTEEN

I wiggled my fingers in the dirt, feeling it jam up under my fingernails. I found another, smaller bone and then a whole group of bones so little they might have been chicken bones. Willie's toes?

I laid all of the bones together on the towel and kept searching. When I had dug with my hands for several minutes without finding any more bones, I used the spade to turn over the dirt at the bottom of the hole.

I unearthed more hunks of rotting wood, but no bones.

I decided I must have found them all. I folded the towel tightly around them and put the bundle in the backpack. I tossed all the rotten wood back into the hole, then threw in the torn plastic bag. I didn't know what else to do with it. I couldn't leave it on the ground, and I had too much in my backpack already. I shoveled most of the dirt back into the hole, leaving enough space for the rest of the daisies.

I stomped the dirt down hard all around the clump of daisies before I emptied the rest of the water from the bucket. Breathing hard, I looked in every direction, relieved to see I was still alone.

I left the bucket at the edge of the cemetery. There was no need to carry it up the hill and back; I'd pick it up on my way home.

I considered leaving the metal box, too, since it added a lot of weight to the backpack, but I suspected that whatever was in the box had value. Otherwise, why would someone go to so much trouble to hide it? I didn't want to leave it sitting around unguarded, even in the empty cemetery.

As I walked away from the graveyard, I felt energized. No one had seen me. The dangerous part of my mission was finished.

"I got them, Willie," I said. "I got all your leg bones."

I thought the least he could do was come to offer his congratulations.

Halfway up the hill between the cemetery and the river, I stopped to rest. The metal box was heavy, and

I wished I didn't have to carry it uphill and back. The hatchet and the shovel weren't light, either.

I took the box out of the backpack and fiddled with the brass lock, which held securely.

"What do you have?" Willie appeared, finally, and sat beside me.

"I found this buried in the grave with your leg," I said. "Do you know what it is?"

"It ain't my leg coffin, that's certain. You'll need a file or a heavy pry bar to open that box without the key."

"Your wooden coffin was rotted, but I think I found all your leg bones."

"Could I see them?"

I laid the towel on the ground and carefully unwrapped the bones.

Willie touched the largest one, running a finger gently down the length of the bone.

"This was a fine leg," he said. "All the years I walked on it I never gave it a thought, but I missed it sorely when it was gone. I didn't appreciate what I had until I lost it."

I wrapped up the bones and put them in the backpack again. "Someone must have used your leg's grave as a hiding place," I said as I slid the metal box in beside the towel.

"Who would bury something with my leg?" He sounded as puzzled as I felt.

I thought of the "five *W*'s" I had learned in school—the questions a news story should answer: Who? What? When? Where? Why? I knew where I'd found the box, but I didn't know who had buried it, what was in it, when it had been put in the grave, or why. Five questions, one answer.

I drank more of my water, then hiked the rest of the way to the river. The sun was high now, and when we emerged from the trees to the open riverbank, the rays beat down on my back. I could almost hear Mom's voice: "You need sunscreen on your face and arms."

I always used to get annoyed at her nagging. Now I missed it. Nobody cared if I read past midnight or if I went to bed without brushing my teeth.

I wondered what she and Steven were doing today. Maybe this afternoon when Aunt Ethel and I got the mail there would be a letter for me.

I set the backpack beside Willie's grave and removed the hatchet. I raised and lowered my shoulders a few times, working out the kinks.

The hatchet cut through the rose branches, but it was slow work; the thorns grabbed my hands as I chopped. I wished I had asked Aunt Ethel for some gloves. I tried pulling my sleeves down over my fingertips, but they didn't stay down.

After I cut off each branch, I used the hatchet as a hook to drag the branch to one side. By the time I got all the brambles off Willie's grave, my hands and wrists were covered with scratches. I wiped the blood on my pant legs and used my teeth to remove one especially large thorn from my thumb.

I picked up the spade and began to dig. The soil here was more sandy than at the cemetery, which made the digging easier.

As I worked, I thought about the metal box. Yesterday I'd told myself it was OK to dig up Willie's leg because I wasn't really taking anything from the grave; I was only moving the bones to a new location.

Now I *had* taken something. The metal box didn't belong there in the first place, but it wasn't Willie's, and it certainly wasn't mine. The excuse I'd practiced, in case I got caught, was "I didn't remove anything except Willie's bones." I couldn't say that anymore.

I had believed that once I dug up the bones and got safely away from the cemetery without being seen, my worries were over. Now I wasn't so sure. I didn't think there was any way I could be linked to the removal of the box, but it made me uneasy all the same. I hoped whoever had buried the box wouldn't discover it was gone until fall, when I was safely back in Minneapolis.

When I'd dug down about two feet, I paused to wipe the sweat from my forehead and to drink some more of my water. Puffy blisters had popped up on both of my palms. I eliminated grave digging from my list of possible future careers.

I wondered how deep I needed to go. I didn't want to dig until I found Willie's skeleton. I was getting used to freaky situations, but that would be too weird even for me. On the other hand, I didn't want to bury the leg so shallow that a dog or coyote would dig up the bones and run off with them.

Willie made the decision for me. He looked into the hole I'd dug and said, "You're deep enough." I don't think he wanted to look at his skeleton, either.

I laid the towel at the edge of the hole, then unwrapped the bones. I lifted one long side of the towel and gently shook it until the bones slid down into the hole. I grabbed the spade and shoveled the dirt back in, quickly covering the bones.

When I had replaced all the dirt I'd removed, I used the hatchet to drag some of the rose brambles back on top of the grave. I heaped them all across the dirt so if anyone happened this way, it wouldn't be obvious that someone had recently been digging here.

When I finished, I looked at Willie. He stood beside the pile of branches, smiling at me. "I've waited a long time for this," he said.

"Do you want to say a prayer or something?" I asked.

He shook his head. "Sarah prayed for me the first time," he said. "Nobody needs two funerals."

"I guess we're done then." I rolled up the towel, put it and the hatchet in my backpack, and slid my arms into the straps.

Willie still stood beside the grave. He removed his miner's hat, then laid it gently beside the pile of branches. I realized Willie wanted a marker for this spot, something permanent like the gravestones in the cemetery.

I thought of Florence's gravestone that said BELOVED DAUGHTER, SISTER, AND TEACHER and wondered what Willie's ought to say. LOVING HUSBAND AND FATHER seemed appropriate, but I knew there would be no such marker.

I wished I had dug up the small W.M.M. plaque and brought it along to identify this grave. I didn't offer to do it now, though. I had dug up the bones and made it out of the cemetery without being seen; the last thing I wanted to do was return to dig up Willie's marker. Especially now, after I'd taken the box from the grave.

After Willie laid his hat on the grave, he noticed me watching.

"Something to mark the spot," he said.

"When you disappear, your hat does, too," I said.

"Only if I'm wearing it. I can leave it here."

"Won't you miss it?" I asked.

He rubbed one hand across the top of his head. "Yes, and I worry someone will take the hat, but it's all I have."

I picked up the shovel and started to walk away, then turned back. "Keep your hat, Willie," I said. "I'll remove the little gravestone with your initials on it, bring it here, and put it in the proper place."

"You are the best friend this old coal miner ever had," Willie said as he put the hat back on.

My arms ached, my back hurt, my legs were sore, and the blisters on my hands were oozing, but I felt good inside. After more than one hundred years, Willie's leg was finally reunited with his body.

CHAPTER FOURTEEN

The straps on the backpack chafed on the way downhill, but my good mood overcame any discomfort. I had done it!

Willie floated beside me, grinning at me all the way.

The sun hid behind gathering clouds. By the time we reached the cemetery, the wind had come up.

I collected the bucket, then headed up the railroad trail. By the time I got to the tree house, every muscle in my body ached. I looked forward to a hot shower and a cold lemonade, but first I wanted to try to pry open the box I'd found.

I didn't see Mrs. Stray or her kittens, but the cat food was gone. I refilled the dish, then climbed up the ladder and sat on the big pillow.

I removed the heavy metal box from my backpack and fiddled with the lock for a minute. It held fast.

Then I remembered the railroad spike in my backpack. I stuck the narrow end of the spike under the box lid, then pressed down as hard as I could on the spike's head. The edge of the metal lid bent slightly. I moved the spike half an inch and tried again. The metal bent there, too. I worked my way methodically along the edge of the box, prying the lid as much as I could.

Around and around the box I went. Each time I pressed on the spike, the box lid gave a tiny bit more. I shoved the spike in as far as I could and pressed with both hands until one side of the lid raised up far enough so I could peek inside.

I held the box up to the window so the light shined inside it. Then I peered into the box and gasped. The box contained money! I couldn't tell if there was a whole stack of paper money or merely a bill on top of something else. I also couldn't tell what denomination the money was. The opening I'd made wasn't wide enough for me to stick my fingers in and pull the money out.

In my excitement, I forgot all about my hunger and thirst and aching muscles. I focused on opening the metal box. I pried the edge of the lid a while longer, trying to loosen the hinges, but I couldn't open it farther. I needed sturdier tools. I'd gone as far as I could go with the old railroad spike.

I left the spade and hatchet outside the tree house, then carried the box to Aunt Ethel's house. Although I was curious about the contents, I was starving, and I needed a shower. I itched where the sweat had trickled down my neck.

I decided to eat first, get cleaned up, then take the box out to the barn, where all the tools were. I'd open it there and see how much money it contained. Maybe it's only play money, I thought. The box might have been buried by kids pretending to be pirates. There might be a pretend treasure map showing the cemetery, with a big *X* on the grave of Willie's leg.

Once I knew for sure what the box held, I would show it to Aunt Ethel. If it contained real money, she could call the police for me. It might be unjust, but a phone call from an adult would be taken more seriously than a call from a kid.

I had already concocted my story to explain how I found the box. I planned to say I went to the cemetery to plant some daisies on Aunt Florence's grave. After I got there, I decided to put a few on one of the other graves, too, so I chose one that looked neglected.

When I dug a hole for the flowers, I discovered the box. I didn't know what it was, but I knew it was too new to have been buried very long. It seemed suspicious, so I brought it home. If it was supposed to be there, I'd take it right back.

The story sounded plausible. There was no reason for anyone not to believe it.

"I'm home!" I called as I set the box on the kitchen table.

The house was still. "Aunt Ethel?"

No answer.

I looked around the kitchen. A large pink bakery-type box sat on the counter next to a sheet cake frosted with white frosting. Yellow roses made of buttercream icing decorated the edges of the cake, but the center part, where it would say "Happy Birthday" or "Congratulations" or whatever it was supposed to say, was still blank. She had not finished the cake.

A tube of frosting with a pointed tip lay on the counter next to the cake. I squeezed the end of the tube, and a line of yellow frosting came out the tip onto my finger. I licked it off.

"Aunt Ethel?" I called again. "Are you here?"

I found her lying on the living room floor. Her eyes were closed, and her face was the color of fireplace ashes. I knelt beside her. "Aunt Ethel?"

She didn't answer.

She was unconscious, but I could tell she was breathing.

I grabbed the phone and called 911. "My aunt needs help," I told the operator. I explained the situation and gave Aunt Ethel's name. "I don't know the street address," I said, "but it's up the hill from Carbon City. It's the first driveway after you pass the cemetery."

"We'll find it," the operator said. "Help is on the way."

Later I learned Carbon City has a volunteer fire department, and the medic unit consists of local people, most of whom had lived in the area all their lives. The only address they needed was "the Hodge place."

By the time I hung up, Aunt Ethel had opened her eyes.

"Are you okay?" I asked. "What happened?"

"I tripped on the edge of the rug."

"I called nine-one-one. There's an ambulance on the way."

"Call them back and tell them not to come. I'll be fine."

She sat up.

"Maybe we should let them come and check you, just to be sure."

"No! They'll want to put me in the hospital. Help me stand up."

When I tried to help her stand, she groaned and

sank back down to the floor. "I sprained my ankle," she said. "Get me a package of peas from the freezer."

I found the peas, thinking it appropriate that Aunt Ethel would use frozen vegetables for an ice pack. "Which ankle?" I asked.

She pointed to her left side, and I placed the frozen peas on that ankle.

Fifteen minutes after I made the call, an ambulance drove in Aunt Ethel's driveway. Two men carrying medical supplies hurried to the door.

"You can leave," she called as I let them in. "I don't need help after all."

"Since we're here, ma'am," one of the medics said, "we're required to examine you."

"Fleas and mosquitoes!" Aunt Ethel said. "All I did was sprain my ankle. I don't need doctors."

Ignoring her protests, the medics listened to Aunt Ethel's heart, took her pulse and blood pressure, and examined the ankle under the bag of peas. One of them said, "I think that ankle's broken. You'll need to go to the hospital in Diamond Hill for an X-ray."

"I'm not going. I hate hospitals."

"If your ankle's broken, ma'am, you'll need to have a cast put on it."

"Mom broke her ankle once," I said. "It healed fine with the cast."

"Without it, you'd be in constant pain and likely not be able to walk right ever again," the medic said. "You don't want to need help to get around, do you?"

"Oh, all right, I'll go. But I'm not staying there. I'm coming straight home as soon as they treat my ankle."

"Is it OK if I go with her?" I asked.

"Are you a relative?" the man asked.

"I'm her nephew, Josh McDowell. I'm visiting her for the summer."

"You can ride along if you want to."

"Yes, I do. Thanks."

I didn't really want to go anywhere. I was tired and hungry. I wanted to stay here, finish opening the metal box, and see if it held real money. But I couldn't let them take Aunt Ethel away by herself. It's scary enough to go to the hospital without being all alone.

I thought of telling the medics about the box, but I didn't know them, and they were busy taking care of Aunt Ethel. One of them put a splint on her ankle to hold it steady, while the other rolled a gurney into the house. I couldn't bother them with my story of a buried box. Besides, I wanted to tell Aunt Ethel before I told anyone else and let her be the one to call the police.

Maybe when we got to the hospital, the doctors would find that her ankle was only sprained, not broken. Probably she would not have to be admitted but would come home today. I thought back to when Mom's ankle was broken. She had not stayed in the hospital, but she'd been on pain medication that made her sleepy for a couple of days. Gramma had come to stay with us for a week.

If Aunt Ethel wasn't able to talk to the police by tomorrow, I'd call them myself. By then, I'd have the box open all the way, and I'd know exactly what I'd found.

"Get my purse, Josh," Aunt Ethel said as the medics lifted her onto the gurney. "I'll need my Medicare card at the hospital."

"What about a house key?" I asked.

"No need. I never lock the house."

While the medics loaded her into the ambulance, I ran upstairs to her bedroom and grabbed her purse.

I had been taught always to lock the house when I left, so I felt around in the purse for a house key but didn't find one. There were two keys on her key ring; one said FORD on it, so I knew that was for her truck, and the other was a small key with USPS on it, plus a number and a warning not to duplicate the key. I figured the letters stood for United States Postal

Service, and the key would open Aunt Ethel's post office box.

I thought back to the night I had arrived—could it be only four days ago? So much had happened, it seemed more like three weeks. I remembered when we got here that first night, Aunt Ethel had walked in without unlocking the door first.

I couldn't be sure that Aunt Ethel would be coming home today, and it made me uneasy to leave the house unlocked, but since I had no key to get back in, I didn't lock up when we left.

One of the medics drove, and the other rode in back with Aunt Ethel so I sat in front. I hoped the driver would turn on a siren and some flashing lights, but he didn't. Maybe they only used the siren and lights in life-and-death cases.

Raindrops spattered the windshield. The driver turned on the windshield wipers.

"Will she be OK?" I asked as we turned out of the driveway.

"A broken ankle's fixable, but every patient is different. She'll probably get a cast and come home tonight or maybe tomorrow. Of course there's always the chance that she'll need a few weeks in a rehab hospital."

I liked the first choice—coming home again right

away. It was best for Aunt Ethel and also best for me. If she had to spend several weeks in a hospital, where would I go? If I had to go somewhere else now, what would happen to Mrs. Stray and her kittens? I didn't want to leave until I'd tamed them and found them homes.

Maybe I could stay in Aunt Ethel's house by myself. I knew Mom and Steven would never allow that, but I wouldn't have to tell them about Aunt Ethel. I could send letters about Carbon City without mentioning that she'd fallen and had to go to the hospital. I could live in her house and ride my bike to the Carbon City Market if I needed supplies. I could take care of the peacock and spend my time taming Mrs. Stray and her three kittens.

For Aunt Ethel's sake, I hoped she'd be fine, but if she wasn't, I could manage on my own. If I got lonely, there was always Willie.

It's pretty strange, I thought, when the only friend I have is a ghost who died more than one hundred years ago. Still, a friend is a friend, and I'd grown fond of the one-legged coal miner.

CHAPTER FIFTEEN

Mr. Turlep had driven the narrow street beside the Carbon City cemetery so many times that he felt his car could practically steer itself. He used to stop on the side of the road for a few minutes and stare at the spot where the money was buried, but for the last few months, he'd been content simply to drive slowly past, savoring the anticipation of his retirement.

On Friday afternoon, he barely glanced at the cemetery, knowing he'd be returning after dark that night to dig up his money. When he was nearly past, his foot slammed on the brake as he swiveled his head to look back.

Someone had planted flowers on the grave. *His* grave! Well, not actually his, of course, but the one he'd chosen.

He had carefully researched all the graves—pretending he was writing an article about local history for a magazine.

He'd selected the grave with only the initials W.M.M. because nobody could remember who was buried there.

Information existed for most of the graves. Even though a fire in 1922 had destroyed all the official records, most of the graves had been identified by surviving relatives, and the names and dates were recorded in the new cemetery book.

Only two of the graves contained unidentified people. Mr. Turlep had chosen the most unkempt of those two graves, the one with the smallest marker. There were only initials on the marker, making it unlikely some long-lost relative would arrive.

In the months since Mr. Turlep had buried his money, there had never been any evidence of a visitor to the grave. Why would someone have come today of all days?

He got out of his car and strode toward the bright patch of yellow daisies. How deep had the person dug? Deep enough to find his box?

Surely anyone planting flowers on a grave would stop digging if their shovel struck metal. Wouldn't they?

Beads of perspiration popped out on Mr. Turlep's brow. He had to know. He dropped to his knees beside the daisies. Grabbing them in his fists, he yanked them up, roots and all, and discarded them on the grass. Then he began digging furiously with his bare hands, clawing at the dirt and pushing it aside until he had a hole so deep his arms were in clear to his elbows.

His fingers closed around something thin and smooth. When he pulled on it, the torn plastic bag pulled loose from the dirt. Mr. Turlep looked at the hole torn in the bag, where the staples had been ripped free. This was the bag that had held his box of money; he was sure of that.

Someone had been here, removed the box, and buried the empty bag in the grave.

As the ambulance approached the cemetery, I saw a car parked on the side of the road. A man knelt on the grass, digging with his hands in the dirt where Willie's leg had been buried! The yellow daisies lay on the grass beside the grave.

My heart leaped to my throat. The man had his back to the road so I didn't see his face. The ambulance driver kept his eyes on the road and seemed not to notice the man.

It had to be the person who had buried the box. Who else would dig in the dirt like a dog, throwing freshly planted flowers aside?

He must have gone to the cemetery, seen the daisies, and known that whoever planted them might have accidentally found the box. Now he would discover that the box was missing.

I had missed him by only a few hours. What if he had come while I was still there, removing Willie's leg bones? Instead of riding to town in an ambulance right now, I'd be riding in a police car.

Calm down, I told myself. He didn't catch me, and he can't find out I took the box. Even if he knows W.M.M. stands for Wilber Michael Martin, there's no way to link me to Willie. I'm not related to him, and neither is Aunt Ethel. I've never been seen at the cemetery. The man will discover the box is gone, but he can't trace it to me.

When we reached the hospital, Aunt Ethel informed everyone she saw that she was not going to stay there.

A nurse whisked Aunt Ethel away to an examining room while an admitting clerk asked me questions about her age and her medical history.

Although I felt foolish carrying a woman's purse, I was glad I had brought it because the clerk did need

Aunt Ethel's Medicare card and another insurance card.

I didn't know Aunt Ethel's birth date, and there was no driver's license in the purse. I had wondered if she had one; now I was certain she didn't.

I couldn't help on medical history, either. I had no idea whether she had been sick or healthy all her life. Eventually the clerk found the information she needed in the computer, from a time ten years earlier when Aunt Ethel had been treated for pneumonia.

The admitting clerk said, "When the doctor finishes examining your aunt, he'll come out to the emergency room waiting area and tell you the diagnosis."

After the paperwork was done, I found a restroom and scrubbed the dirt and sweat from my hands and face. Then I sat in the emergency waiting room. My stomach growled from hunger, but I didn't see any vending machines, and I didn't want to leave the waiting room to look for a place to eat for fear I'd miss the doctor.

Someone had left a newspaper in the waiting room, and I skimmed the headlines without reading the stories. I began to imagine the next day's headlines: BOY DIES OF HUNGER IN HOSPITAL WAITING ROOM.

The minutes crawled past. I fidgeted, thinking about the box I'd found and the man I'd seen at the cemetery. I had left all the doors unlocked and the box on the kitchen table. What if it was full of real money? What if someone went in Aunt Ethel's house and found it?

I should have hidden it before I left. Why didn't I think of that? I could have stuck it in the freezer or put it inside my pillowcase or in the clothes washer—anyplace but sitting on the table in plain sight.

What if the medics told their families or co-workers how they'd taken Ethel Hodge to the hospital? Someone might go to Aunt Ethel's house. Her friends probably knew she never locked the door. They'd walk right in and see the box and wonder what was in it.

How could I have been so stupid as to leave the box unguarded? My imagination took off like a batter who'd laid down a perfect bunt. A bum could knock on the door, asking for work or a handout, and when nobody answered, he'd go inside and find the box. The newspaper delivery person might come to collect for this month's papers—and leave with the box.

The longer I waited for the doctor, the more certain I became that by the time I got back to Aunt Ethel's house, the metal box and its contents would be gone. I would never find out what it contained or who it belonged to.

We had arrived at the hospital at 4:45. By 5:30, I couldn't sit still. My nerves jangled each time a doctor was paged, and I jumped when anyone passed by in the hall. I paced around the waiting room, glancing at the wall clock every few minutes. 5:45. 5:50.

New headlines scrolled across my mind: VANDALS TRASH UNLOCKED HOUSE. BOY CLAIMS MYSTERY BOX IS STOLEN.

At six-thirty, a man wearing white scrubs came out. "Are you waiting for Miss Hodge?" he asked.

"Yes. How is she?"

"I'm Dr. Baker. Are your parents here?" He looked around, obviously hoping to discuss Aunt Ethel's condition with an adult.

I said, "They aren't here right now." That was true, even though I knew he meant were they here in the hospital with me. I added, "I'm her nephew."

"Your aunt has a broken ankle; we've put a cast on it. I don't anticipate problems from it, but she's sleepy from the pain medication I gave her. I want her to stay here overnight so we can watch her. The ankle should heal fine, but her foot needs to stay elevated for a few days."

"Do you think she can go home tomorrow?"

"There's no way to know for sure, son. Your aunt is not the most cooperative patient. Are your parents coming right back? I'd like to speak to them."

"They'll be gone a while, but I'll tell them what you said." Eventually.

"I have another emergency case coming in. Your parents can talk to a nurse if they have questions. Miss Hodge is being put in room two-thirteen. Second floor."

"Is it OK if I go see her?"

"Wait until your parents return; then go with them." Dr. Baker hurried off to tend to his other patient.

I found an elevator and rode to the second floor. As I followed the room number signs, I passed the nurses' station. A nurse standing behind the counter said, "Visitors under age sixteen aren't allowed unless they're with an adult."

"My great-aunt's in room two-thirteen," I said. "I rode here in the ambulance with her, and I have her purse." I held it up. "Could I go in for a minute to give it to her? I promise I won't stay."

"Are you with an adult?"

"No. I'm the only one here with Aunt Ethel."

"How old are you?"

"Thirteen." Well, I'd be thirteen next month; that was close enough. I gave her my most pleading look. "Please? I feel goofy carrying a lady's purse around."

The woman's stern expression softened. "Go ahead," she said. "Take out any money and credit cards before you leave the purse. Your aunt won't need money here, and there's no use tempting a dishonest person."

"You think someone might steal from a sick person in the hospital?" That seemed about as low as anyone could get.

"It's happened," the nurse replied. "Don't stay more than a few minutes."

"I won't. Thanks for letting me go in."

"Me? I never saw you." She busied herself with the medicine cart; I walked past the nurses' station and entered Aunt Ethel's room.

She lay in bed, her left foot propped on a pillow. Her eyes were closed.

"Aunt Ethel?" I whispered.

Her eyes stayed shut. I decided not to wake her up. If I did, she'd only demand to go home.

I opened the purse. Aunt Ethel didn't have a credit card, but I removed eighteen dollars and forty-five cents, along with the key chain. I wanted to be able to get the mail out of the post office box.

I put the purse in the drawer of the bedside stand. Even though I'd taken out the money, she might need the comb, pencil and notebook, or handkerchief that the purse still contained.

I waited a couple of minutes, wondering if Aunt Ethel would wake up. When she didn't, I whispered, "I'll take care of Florence while you're in the hospital." I didn't know if she could hear me or not, but I figured Florence was the one thing she'd worry about.

I left her room and headed for the elevator.

When I got back to the lobby, I realized I had no way to get home. The medics had left as soon as they'd delivered Aunt Ethel, and I didn't know anyone in Diamond Hill or in Carbon City. Except for Aunt Ethel and the hospital staff, the only person I'd talked to in the entire state of Washington was the man in the Carbon City Market, and I didn't know his name. He didn't know mine, either. There was nobody I could call to ask for a ride home.

Although I'd spent the last hour imagining hordes of people swarming to Aunt Ethel's house, the only friend she had mentioned was Muriel. I didn't know Muriel's last name or where she lived.

I knew if I explained my dilemma to the admitting clerk, she would probably find someone to help me, but I didn't want anyone to know my plan to stay at Aunt Ethel's house alone until she got out of the hospital.

I found a pay phone with a local directory chained to it, then looked up taxis in the Yellow Pages. It listed only one company. I dialed the number and asked how much it would cost to go from the Diamond Hill Hospital to the far side of Carbon City.

"Ten dollars."

"OK. Can you come now?"

Five minutes later, a yellow-and-blue taxi pulled up. The driver wore a white turban and spoke halting English, but he understood when I said Carbon City.

My mind raced in circles as we drove, the way Charlie used to chase his tail. What a day! I'd never ridden in a cab before, much less an ambulance. I'd never helped a ghost, or dug up bones from a grave, or found a buried box. No wonder I was weary. I'd never stayed alone overnight, either, and that part was yet to come.

The taxi driver slowed when he drove into Carbon City. "Keep going," I said. "It's up the hill a couple more miles."

As the taxi approached the cemetery, I leaned forward in my seat, looking for a car. It was gone. The daisies still lay in the grass; the man who had pulled them out had not bothered to replant them.

I wondered if I should call the police as soon as I got home. From the frantic way that man had been digging, the box I'd removed must contain something valuable. But if it did, why would he have buried it in the cemetery? If it was full of money, as I suspected, why wouldn't he have deposited it in the bank? It didn't earn interest underground.

A new thought hit me. What if the box had been stolen? Maybe it didn't belong to this man, and he'd buried it to keep it hidden until he thought it was safe to open it.

I decided to force open the box all the way, find out exactly what it contained, and then call the police immediately.

I was thinking so hard about the man at the cemetery and the mysterious box, I nearly missed Aunt Ethel's road. At the last second, I said, "Turn there," and the taxi swerved onto the gravel driveway.

When we reached the house, the driver looked at the meter. "Ten dollars," he said. "Long way out here. Long way back."

I wondered if I was supposed to tip him. It *was* a long drive for the taximan, and he would be going back without a passenger. I gave the driver twelve dollars, which seemed to please him.

As soon as I got in the house, I rushed to the

kitchen. The box sat on the table, exactly where I'd left it. Relieved, I opened the fridge. It was past eight o'clock, and I'd eaten only an apple all day. I was so hungry I would have eaten spinach or Brussels sprouts, but I didn't have to. I found a pork chop, some fried potatoes, and green beans, left over from yesterday's breakfast.

Wishing Aunt Ethel had a microwave, I wrapped my meal in foil and put it in the oven to heat.

While I waited for my dinner to get warm, I ate three chocolate chip cookies. Dessert first never killed anybody; that's my motto.

I was sorely tempted to have a slice of the unfinished cake, but I didn't. I wondered if Aunt Ethel's customer had come while I was at the hospital, then left when no one answered the door.

Three times I opened the oven and stuck my finger inside the foil to see if my dinner was hot. On the third try I gave up and ate everything lukewarm. Even after the cookies, I was too hungry to wait any longer. How did Aunt Ethel survive without a microwave? I would have made a rotten pioneer.

I ate right out of the foil. One less dish to wash. I washed my fork and glass, then picked up the metal box and headed for the barn.

CHAPTER SIXTEEN

Breathing hard, Mr. Turlep held the torn plastic bag and stared into the empty hole.

The box was gone. The box containing all the money for his golden retirement had been stolen.

How dare someone remove what belonged to him?

He knew the box had been discovered accidentally because he had told no one where he'd hidden it. Unfortunately, he did not know whose grave this was, so he had no way to track down any relative or friend who might have planted the daisies.

Mr. Turlep stood up, wiped his filthy hands on his suit pants, and looked around the cemetery. The same kind of daisies bloomed on another grave a few rows over. The thief must have planted those, too.

Mr. Turlep rushed over to the second clump of

daisies and read the name on the headstone. FLORENCE HODGE. He remembered her; she and her sister used to come to the bank to complain whenever interest rates on savings went down. Mr. Turlep didn't know she had died, but, come to think of it, he had not seen her in a while.

Was the sister still living? Had she come here and planted flowers? Is that who took his money? If so, it ought to be a simple matter to get it back, as long as he got to the old woman before she told anyone what she'd found.

Mr. Turlep ran back to his car and broke the speed limit driving toward town. He tried to remember the sister's name. Edna? Emma? He decided to go to the Carbon City Post Office and ask where the Hodge sisters lived. The surviving sister might still live around here. In a small town like Carbon City, everyone would use the same post office.

He reached the post office as a woman was turning a key in the lock on the front door. He screeched to a halt in the parking lot and jumped out of his car.

"Sorry," she said. "The post office is closed for today. If you need stamps, you'll have to come back tomorrow."

"All I need is information. I'm looking for the sister of an old friend. My friend's name was Florence

Hodge, but I can't remember the name of her sister or where she lives."

"I'm not the regular postmistress," the woman said. "She was sick today, and I substituted for her. I don't sub here often, so I don't know the local people. If there is a Hodge who has a P.O. box, I wouldn't know the street address. If you want to come back tomorrow morning, the regular post-mistress will be back, and she might be able to help you."

"Can't you look it up? You must have records."

"Sorry. The post office closed at five; I stayed to finish some paperwork." The woman walked to her car, ignoring the icy glare from Mr. Turlep.

He went next door to the Carbon City Market and asked the clerk if he could use a telephone directory.

The man reached under the counter and began sorting through piles of papers. "You want King County or Pierce County?" he asked.

"I want this area. The local numbers."

"Hold on, then. It's in the back room by my personal phone."

Mr. Turlep drummed his fingers on the counter while the man ambled to the rear of the store and went through a door marked PRIVATE.

"Don't take all day," Mr. Turlep called after him. "I'm in a hurry!"

The clerk reappeared. "Keep your shirt on," he grumbled as he slapped the slim phone book on the counter.

Mr. Turlep turned quickly to the *H* page and ran his finger down the listings. He stopped at *E. Hodge.* A phone number followed but no address.

"It doesn't give the address," he said.

"Who is it you're trying to find?"

Mr. Turlep hesitated. He didn't want to tell this man he was searching for someone named Hodge, whose first name he didn't know. What if the old lady put up a struggle and wouldn't give him the box? What if he had to take it by force? It was foolish to have a witness who could identify him, a witness who would swear he had come in the market looking for Miss Hodge's address.

It would be better to drive to the bank and look through the records there. Most of the old-timers who lived around here had stuck with the local bank, even after two of the big national banks opened branches in town. Probably this Hodge woman's address was on file in his own office, where nobody would wonder why he wanted it.

Mr. Turlep slapped the phone book closed, then

turned and pushed open the door. As he hurried out, he heard the clerk call, "You're welcome!"

He headed away from Carbon City, back to the bank in Diamond Hill. As he drove, he became more and more agitated. What if the woman had already called the police and turned the money in? What if he was already too late?

He had never bothered to wipe his fingerprints off the metal box before he put it in the bag because he'd been positive it would never be found. He wondered how long fingerprints stay on a surface. Could they still be lifted from the box? Maybe it was good that the Hodge woman had taken the plastic bag off. Now her fingerprints were on the box, too, on top of his.

As he reached the city limits of Diamond Hill, a sleek black cat dashed across the road in front of his car. Mr. Turlep slammed on his brakes, made a U-turn, and drove four blocks out of his way to avoid driving where the cat had crossed. He wasn't superstitious, he told himself, but why take chances?

He reached the bank, punched in the alarm code, and used the back entrance. He booted up his computer, opened the list of customer files, and scrolled down until he reached Hodge.

There she was! Ethel Hodge. She had a checking account, where a Social Security check was deposited automatically on the third of every month. She also had a small certificate of deposit. No wonder he didn't remember her first name. Even though she had been a bank customer for more than fifty years, she'd never taken out a loan, and she had minimal assets. Mr. Turlep only paid attention to his wealthier clients.

Both the checking account and the certificate of deposit gave the Carbon City post office box as the address. Nowhere in the bank's records could he find the physical address. Where did this woman live?

He closed the current customer file and opened the file called Closed Accounts. This time he searched for Florence Hodge, but the information was the same—nothing but a post office box. He'd have to go back to the Carbon City Market and ask that slow-moving clerk to give him directions.

Mr. Turlep closed the files, turned off the computer, reset the bank alarm, and locked the door. But he didn't drive straight back to Carbon City. Instead, he went to his apartment. Now that he'd had time to think about it, he realized it was crucial for him to leave for Florida that night, as soon as he had the money. He couldn't take a chance that the Hodge woman would keep quiet—or the market clerk, for that matter.

Since he had planned to go the next day, his bags were already packed. He would leave the boxes for Goodwill and the load of trash for the dump in his apartment. Let the landlord deal with it.

He hurried inside and opened his bedroom closet. He removed a box, set it on his bed, opened it, and took out dozens of back issues of *Deep-Sea Fishing* magazine. At the bottom of the box lay a black ski mask and a handgun, the ones he'd used the night two years ago when he stole the money.

He'd bought the ski mask at a garage sale a few weeks before he used it. The handgun came from a gun shop in Tacoma, one with a reputation for not requiring background checks and for "losing" guns to theft. Customers who paid cash for a gun did so with the assurance there would never be a way to trace that gun back to the purchaser. Mr. Turlep had paid cash.

He had hidden the gun and the ski mask under the magazines as soon as he got home the night of the robbery, and he had intended never to touch either of them again. His plan had been to take several boxes of clothing and household items to a Goodwill donation station tomorrow morning before he left town for good. By the time someone discovered one of the boxes contained items other than magazines, he would already be halfway to Florida—and nobody would even know where the items had come from.

Now he carried the gun and ski mask back to his car, hid them under the seat, and drove the eighteen miles back to Carbon City.

It was long past Mr. Turlep's dinner hour, and his hunger made him irritable.

When he entered the Market, the clerk said, "Oh. You again."

"I forgot something," Mr. Turlep said.

"Your manners?"

"I forgot to ask you for directions. I'm trying to find Ethel Hodge. Do you know where she lives?"

"Up the hill about six miles. The old Hodge place. Go past the cemetery and then keep going until the paved road ends and the gravel road starts. You'll see her driveway on the right."

"I didn't know there were any homes beyond the cemetery."

"There's only the one. It's been there forever; the parents homesteaded the place. The two girls grew up there and then stayed on after the old folks died. One sister's gone now, too—Florence, God rest her soul. But Ethel's still alive and kicking as far as I know, though I haven't seen her in a while. She bakes cakes for all the big events around here. You haven't lived until you've tasted Ethel Hodge's lemon layer cake."

Mr. Turlep couldn't wait while the man yammered on about the Hodge woman's cakes. He walked away while the man was in mid-sentence and rushed to his car. As the market door banged shut, he heard the man holler, "You're welcome again!"

Impudent clerk. Didn't he know he was insulting the manager of the bank? Let him come in next week wanting a loan so he could buy a new car. Mr. Turlep began imagining how he'd turn down the application, then realized he would no longer have any say about who got loans and who didn't. Today had been his last day of work, his last day to earn a paycheck. He gripped the steering wheel and started up the hill. He had to get the box of money.

He drove past the cemetery again. The rain fell steadily now. He had never come here after dark before, but his eyes automatically looked toward the place where his money had been hidden. His headlights illuminated the wilted daisies that lay beside the gaping hole.

He continued up the hill and found the road that the clerk had described. A small wooden sign on a post said HODGE.

Mr. Turlep stopped as soon as he turned into the driveway. He put the ski mask on, then he loaded the gun and laid it in his lap. He drove slowly down the long, winding driveway, anger boiling inside him like hot lava, ready to erupt.

An old truck sat at the end of the driveway. He saw no other cars. Good. She must be alone.

The old woman was probably trying to open the box. He'd show her the gun and tell her the box belonged to him. She'd hand it over without a word. She'd better, because he intended to do whatever he had to do to get the money back.

There were no neighbors out here, no houses for miles. No one would hear if a gun went off.

CHAPTER SEVENTEEN

I rummaged through the tools in the barn until I found a sturdy metal file. I jammed it in the opening I'd made between the lid and the box itself. I sawed the file back and forth, trying to cut through the hinges.

When that didn't work, I used a pry bar to work the hinges loose. I stuck the pry bar under a hinge, then hit the pry bar with a hammer. The hinge gave a little, so I did it again and again. Each time, the hinge loosened a bit more.

Darkness fell early because of the rain. I turned on the single light that hung from a chain and kept prying.

It took me nearly an hour of steady work, but the hinges finally broke loose. I could open the box from the back side, even though it was still locked. I held the box under the light and looked at its contents: money. Lots of money.

I lifted out a pile of crisp new paper bills held together with a narrow paper band. This was not Monopoly money, buried by children playing pirate games. These bills were real.

A one-hundred-dollar bill was on top. I slid it out and held it toward the lightbulb. Last year my social studies teacher had talked about the U.S. Bureau of Printing and Engraving, the government agency that makes our money. He showed the class how to check for counterfeit twenty-dollar bills by holding the money up to a light. He said when we did, we should be able to see a face that didn't show before. He had passed a twenty-dollar bill around, and we each got a turn to hold it up to the light and find the secret face.

When I held the one-hundred-dollar bill toward the barn light, I couldn't see an extra face. I tried to recall what my teacher had said. Did the test only work on twenties?

Still holding the bill up to the light, I moved it to a different angle, and that's when I remembered. My teacher had not demonstrated a one-hundred-dollar bill, but he'd told us about a special ink that's used on the numerals in the bottom right-hand corner when one-hundred-dollar bills are printed. As I tilted the bill, the number 100 in that corner changed from green to black. I moved the bill back and forth, watching the numeral turn green, then black again.

The money was not fake; it was real.

I used my thumb to flip through the edges of the rest of the bills in the stack, looking at the number in the corner of each one. All of the bills were the same.

I counted: There were one hundred bills in this stack. One hundred times one hundred dollars . . . I held ten thousand dollars in one hand!

I couldn't get the bill I'd removed to slide back under the strip of paper so I laid it on top and set that stack of bills on the floor. I took out another stack, and then another, counting the bills in each one.

Some of the stacks at the bottom were held together with green rubber bands, and the bills were worn, as if they'd been in circulation for a while. Those stacks were slightly thicker, but each one held the same amount.

Altogether, the box contained thirteen stacks of bills, with ten thousand dollars in each stack!

I did the math in my head. Oh, man! Along with Willie's leg bones, I had removed one hundred thirty thousand dollars from the grave!

Wait a minute. The amount sounded familiar. Aunt Ethel had told me that's how much the Cash for Critters auction had raised. One hundred thirty thousand dollars had been stolen by the masked robber outside the bank.

Could this be the money the community had raised for the animal shelter? In my mind, I replayed Aunt Ethel's account of the robbery. I was sure she had said bags of money were stolen.

The bags from the auction would have contained bills of many sizes, not all one-hundred-dollar bills. Still, the amount seemed suspicious. The thief could have exchanged any coins and lesser bills for bills this size, so the money would fit in a smaller box and be easier to hide.

Shaking with excitement, I stuffed the money back in the box, pulled the light chain, and carried the box out of the barn.

The sky and yard were black as midnight now, although the rain had stopped. A crescent moon peeked over the treetops, too slim to send any light to the ground. It didn't matter. I knew where the house was, and I ran toward it, clutching the box of money in my arms.

I was halfway to the back door when headlights announced a car coming down the driveway. I stopped, my heart pounding. I wanted to shout the news of my discovery to the world, but not everyone is honest. I didn't want to tell the wrong person, especially when I was alone out here in the country.

This car's driver was probably some friend of Aunt Ethel, come to check on me, but I decided to hide the box before I showed myself.

Instead of continuing to the kitchen door, I ran to the big lilac bush near the side of the house and knelt behind it. From there I could see the end of the driveway and the front of the house. I put the box on the ground, shoving it in close to where the lilac branches came out of the dirt.

The car drove in fast. The driver left the lights on when he got out, probably so he could see to walk to the front door.

I started to stand up, intending to go greet the visitor, but when I looked at the driver, my breath caught in my throat.

The driver wore a black ski mask, the kind that covers the whole head, with slits for the eyes and mouth.

This was no friendly visitor.

Why would anyone approach Aunt Ethel's house in the middle of June dressed like that? The only reason I could think of for someone to hide his face with a ski mask was if he intended to commit a crime and didn't want to be recognized.

It seemed too much of a coincidence for this man to come tonight. Did he know Aunt Ethel wasn't here? I wondered if some dishonest hospital employee passed along to a thief the names of people who were admitted to the hospital, knowing the person's house would probably be unattended. If unscrupulous people stole from patients in the hospital, anything was possible.

I dropped back behind the lilac bush, the wet leaves brushing my face.

The man strode quickly up the porch steps, then pounded on the door. "Ethel Hodge!" he called. "Open up!"

Whoever he was, he didn't know Aunt Ethel was in the hospital. If he intended to rob Aunt Ethel, he wouldn't call out her name. But why else would he wear a ski mask in the middle of June? Nothing made sense.

Maybe when nobody answered the door, the man would leave. As soon as he did, I would call the police. I wished I had called them when I first got home from the hospital.

He didn't leave. Instead, he opened the front door and stepped inside. The indoor lights went on.

Through the windows, I could see the man go from room to room. He looked under the table and behind the couch, as if he were searching for something in particular.

Was he looking for the box of money? I couldn't tell if this was the same man I'd seen digging in the cemetery, but even if he was, how could he possibly know I had the box?

Light blazed from the upstairs windows. As I pictured the masked man going into the bedrooms, I realized he would soon discover Aunt Ethel did not live here alone.

I had left my dirty clothes in a pile on the floor. My extra sneakers stood beside the bed. My CDs were stacked on the small table, and a half-read book and a bag of jelly beans rested on the nightstand. It would be perfectly clear that someone besides an eighty-three-year-old woman lived in this house. Someone my age.

Was he a petty thief, looking for anything of value? Or was he the man I'd seen at the cemetery, looking for the box of money?

The upstairs lights went out, followed by the kitchen light, and, last, the living room light. The front door opened. The man returned to his car.

He drove off, spinning his tires in the gravel so it flew toward the porch.

I waited a minute to be sure he was gone. Then I grabbed the box from under the bush, raced toward the house, bolted up the steps, and pushed open the front door.

I flipped the light switch, then ran to Aunt Ethel's old black dial telephone, the one I'd used to call the medics. I put the box on the table and picked up the receiver.

My hands shook as I dialed the numbers. I was probably setting a new record, calling 911 twice in one day from the same telephone.

I held the receiver to my ear. There was no sound. My call had not gone through. I jiggled my finger on the button, then listened again. Nothing. No dial tone.

My eyes followed the telephone cord to where it met the wall. It stopped two feet short; the cord had been cut.

I stood with the useless receiver in my hand, staring at the dangling cord. I was completely isolated. No phone, no neighbors, no way to get help.

I couldn't stay here alone until morning, not with so much money. What if the masked man returned?

I would have to ride the old bicycle down the hill to Carbon City in the dark, using a flashlight to see the road.

I didn't think I could manage to hold a flashlight and the box of money, too, while I rode, so I decided to leave the box here. I grabbed it, ran to the kitchen, and stuck it in the clothes washer.

I raced back to the living room for the flashlight that Aunt Ethel kept next to her recliner in case the power went out. I bent to pick it up when, behind me, I heard a *click* as the front door opened.

I whirled around.

The man in the ski mask stood inside the door. He had a gun in one hand, pointed at me.

"Where's the box?" he asked.

"Box? What box? I don't know what you mean."

"I think you do. You or Ethel Hodge dug up a box at the cemetery today. It's mine, and I want it back. Now."

I tried to look innocent. "What makes you think we have it?"

"Because the flowers planted there are the same as the ones on Florence Hodge's grave. They're all along the side of this house, too. Either you have the box or Ethel Hodge has it. Where is she?"

"She'll be back any minute," I said. I couldn't let him know the truth, that I was here alone.

"Did she take the box with her?"

I stalled, trying to think what to do. "We don't have any box. She, um, went to a neighbor's house."

I remembered Aunt Ethel's gun, the one she had used to shoot the bat. She kept it in her bedroom. Should I pretend the box was upstairs, tell the man I would get it, and then get the gun instead? But I didn't know anything about guns. I wouldn't know how to tell if it was loaded, and even if I did know how to use it, did I really want to shoot at a person? There had to be a better way to save myself than by getting into a gunfight.

A flash of light beamed through the front window. Another car was driving toward the house! The man and I both looked out.

"Here's Aunt Ethel now," I said, as I wondered who it was.

The man stepped close to me. The gun was only a foot from my chest.

"I'll wait behind the couch," he said. "If this is not Ethel Hodge, you will get rid of whoever it is without saying one word about me or about the box you found. Is that clear?"

"I didn't find any . . ."

"Is that clear?" His eyes bore into me through the slits in the ski mask.

I nodded.

"If you don't do as I say, you won't live to see tomorrow."

He pulled the couch out from the wall far enough to get behind it, then he dropped to his knees. I couldn't see him, but I knew he was watching, and I knew the gun was still aimed at me.

There was a quick knock on the door. Then it opened a crack, and a woman's voice called, "Ethel? It's me. I've come for the cake." Without waiting for a response, a woman in a gray pantsuit pushed the door open and stepped inside. A big red hat gave her a cheery look.

"Hello," I said, trying to sound normal. "I'm Josh, Ethel's nephew. She had to leave for a minute. She'll be right back."

The woman frowned. "Ethel doesn't usually drive after dark," she said. "Is everything all right?"

"Oh, yes." I forced a smile. "Everything's fine."

She gave me an odd look, as if she weren't convinced. "Where did she go?"

I blurted the first thing that entered my mind. "A

friend in Carbon City fell and needed some—some pain medicine. Aunt Ethel took her a bottle of Tylenol." I held my breath, hoping the woman wouldn't ask more questions.

"I wonder why she didn't call me," the woman said. "Well, I'm running late as it is. I should have been here hours ago. I tried to call earlier, but nobody answered so I took a chance and came. I saw your lights and knew you were still up. I'm Muriel Morris, by the way, Ethel's friend from Diamond Hill. I ordered a cake for my daughter's birthday. It's tomorrow, but I need to get the cake tonight."

I almost told her the cake wasn't finished, but when I thought about the blank space on the cake and the tube of frosting, I had an idea.

"I can get the cake for you," I said. "It's in the kitchen, all ready to go."

"Oh, thank you, Josh. I'll write out the check while you get it." Muriel sat on the couch, opened her purse, and took out a checkbook. "Whose car is out there?" she asked.

Pretending not to hear her, I hurried to the kitchen. I picked up the tube of frosting and squeezed hard on the bottom. A line of yellow frosting squirted out.

In the middle of the cake, where it was supposed

to say *Happy Birthday,* I made giant frosting letters: *H E L P.* Then I put the cake in the box, shut the box, and carried it into the living room.

From the corner of my eye, I could see the man watching me from behind the couch.

"Aunt Ethel always asks her customers to look at the cake before they take it," I said, "to be sure it's OK."

I started to open the box.

"Oh, I'm sure it's fine," the woman said. "I've been getting cakes from Ethel for years and years. My daughter always wants one on her birthday. Carrot cake."

"I'll be in trouble with Aunt Ethel if I don't show it to you," I said. "Please take a quick look to be sure it's what you ordered."

Keeping my back to the couch, I opened the top of the cake box and thrust the box toward her.

Muriel Morris glanced at the cake. "Oh," she said as she looked more closely.

Don't give me away, I pleaded silently. Please, please don't say anything about the message on the cake.

CHAPTER EIGHTEEN

Mrs. Morris looked at me, then back at the cake.

I closed the box. "I hope it's right," I said. "I know it's important for the cake to say exactly what you want."

"It looks perfect," she said. "Here's the check for your aunt." She gave me the check, and I gave her the cake box. "Tell Ethel I'll call her," Muriel said.

Did she emphasize the words *I'll call* or did I imagine that?

She carried the cake to her car and drove off.

As soon as I heard the car leave, the man came out from behind the couch.

"I notice the knees of your pants are all dirty," he said. "Looks as if you've been kneeling in the dirt, digging."

"I did some gardening for my aunt."

"Yes, you did," he said. "You planted flowers at the cemetery. Where's my box?"

"I told you, I don't know anything about a box."

"I do not have time to play games. I'm going to count to ten. Either you give me the box before I reach ten, or else."

He didn't finish the sentence. He didn't need to. I knew exactly what *or else* meant.

He stepped closer. The overhead light glinted off the barrel of the gun. I couldn't give him the box of money. No matter what he said, it didn't belong to him.

But I couldn't let him shoot me, either.

"One," the man said.

"Willie!" I shouted. "Help me!" I didn't know if the ghost would hear me or if he could do anything to help me; I yelled for help because I didn't know what else to do.

"Quiet!" the man said. "There's no one to hear you. Stop trying to trick me."

"Willie, please!" I yelled. "Hurry!"

Over the man's shoulder, I saw a coal miner's hat. Willie materialized inside the house.

"Drop the gun!" Willie said.

The man did not react.

"He can't hear you," I said.

The man looked behind him, then turned back toward me. I knew he couldn't see the ghost. "Two," he said.

"Willie, he's going to kill me!"

"I told you to quit trying to fool me. There's nobody here."

"Willie's here. My friend."

"Imaginary friend. Three."

Willie put both hands on the telephone and shoved. The phone clattered from its stand to the floor.

The man jumped. "Who did that?" he demanded, looking all around the room.

"My friend," I said. "He's a ghost."

"Ghost!"

"This house is haunted. The ghost's name is Willie, and he wants you to leave."

"I don't believe in ghosts. That's nonsense. Four."

"You'd better do what Willie says. He's a mean, vindictive ghost, and he doesn't like weapons. The last time someone brought a gun in here, Willie disconnected the brakes on the man's car, and they failed as he drove down the hill. If you don't go right now, he'll do the same to you—or worse." I surprised myself with that story. In my desperation, the words rolled effortlessly out of my mouth like a bike going downhill.

The man glanced around the room. I couldn't see his expression because of the mask, but I knew I was making him uneasy.

"Five."

Willie floated across the room to Aunt Ethel's plate rail and pushed a blue-and-white plate off. It crashed to the floor, scattering pieces of pottery across the room.

The hand holding the gun began to shake.

"The ghost is my friend," I said. "If you hurt me, you'll be haunted for the rest of your life. Willie will follow you and cause trouble. You'll live in fear forever!"

Dark blotches of perspiration appeared on the man's shirt under his arms.

"You can't scare me. Six!" His voice got louder, but it lacked the conviction he'd had earlier. My comments about the ghost were scaring him, no matter how much he denied it.

Keep it up, Willie. Throw something else on the floor. If we can stall long enough, the police might come. I didn't know for sure that Muriel Morris had understood my message, but I thought she had.

Otherwise, she would have said the writing on the cake was wrong.

I hoped she had driven to the nearest telephone in Carbon City, called the police, and asked them to go to Ethel Hodge's house immediately. If she had done so, help should be on the way. I had to keep the man from getting his hands on the money until the police arrived—and I had to keep him from shooting me.

"The ghost says you're supposed to go right now," I said. "Forget the box. I don't have it anyway. The ghost says to leave and don't come back."

The man's head turned; his eyes swept all around the room as if he wondered what would fall to the floor next. He even looked up at the ceiling fan.

"This is your last chance," the man said. "I won't shoot if you give me my box. The choice is yours." His voice quavered now, but he still said, "Seven!"

I knew Willie had him frightened, but I couldn't take a chance that he would kill me. I had no way to know when the police would arrive or even IF they would arrive. In a rural area like this, the police probably cover a lot of territory. Even if they responded quickly to Mrs. Morris's call, they could be miles away.

Willie tried to push another plate from the plate rail, but it didn't move. I remembered him saying he couldn't carry the spade because he had little strength. It must have required a huge effort for him to push the telephone and the first plate to the floor; now he couldn't move anything else.

"Eight!"

Willie disappeared through the front door. Why would he leave me now? Even if he couldn't move any more objects, I needed him for moral support. I wanted to shout, "No, Willie! Don't go!" but I couldn't, because I didn't want the man to know Willie had left.

"Nine."

I couldn't let the man get to ten. No amount of money was worth giving up my life for.

I walked slowly to the kitchen, with the man following me.

Hurry! I pleaded, sending my thoughts to the police. Please, please, hurry.

I stopped in front of the clothes washer, listening for any sound of a vehicle approaching Aunt Ethel's house. I heard only the rapid, nervous breathing of the man who held the gun.

"I'll do it," he said. "I'll pull the trigger when I say ten, and when your aunt gets home, I'll pull it again."

I opened the washer and removed the metal box.

As soon as he saw it, he lunged toward me and ripped the box out of my hands. "I knew you had it, you lying little thief. It's my money, for my retirement, and you tried to steal it."

I wanted to shout, "You're the thief! You're the one who stole this money!" but I knew it wasn't smart to make him any angrier than he already was so I said nothing.

"You broke open my locked box. For all I know, you took some of my money."

"It's all there," I said. "You can see for yourself; the box is full. Count it if you don't believe me." I hoped he would; that would take some time, and the police might still get here before he got away.

He opened the lid, looked inside, then shut the box again.

He looked at me for a long moment. "I'm sorry to do this," he said, "but you're the only one who knows about the money." He kept the gun pointed at my chest. "I've waited two years for this day. I can't leave a witness who can identify me and spoil all my plans."

My throat tightened. He was going to shoot me even though he had the money. What a rotten liar!

I tried to stay calm. "I can't identify you," I said. "I have no clue who you are. You've had a mask on the whole time, and I don't live around here so I don't recognize your voice. I'm visiting my aunt. I don't know anybody in this area."

He hesitated, as if thinking over what I'd said. "Why take a chance by leaving a live witness?" he asked. He spoke quietly now, as if he were asking himself, not me.

"If you shoot me," I said, "you won't get away with it. Willie will lead the police to you."

The man looked over his shoulder. "There is no ghost."

"No? Who do you think broke the plate and moved the phone? You can't see him, but my aunt can, and so can her friend. Willie will follow you and tell them where you are, and the police will find you. You'll spend the rest of your life in prison."

I could tell the talk of a ghost made him nervous. While I tried to think how else I could convince him not to kill me, Florence screamed from the porch. It was the loudest, most shrill scream he'd ever made. Even though I knew it was him, I still jumped and got goose bumps on my arms.

Had Willie shown himself to Florence? Is that why he was screeching? He usually only screamed when he spread his train before meals, but Aunt Ethel had told me peacocks also display their feathers and cry out when enemies are near. Maybe Florence regarded Willie as an enemy. Maybe that's why Willie had left me with the man; he'd gone to search for the peacock. Had he been keeping his word about letting the peacock see him, or was he purposely trying to scare Florence into screeching?

The man in the ski mask jumped, too, when Florence screamed. Then he pointed the gun toward the front door. "What was that? Who's out there?"

"It's the last person who didn't do what the ghost told him to do," I said. "Now he's gone mad. He roams through the woods, screaming with fear. That will happen to you if you take the box of money when Willie told you not to. Even worse will happen if you shoot me."

The man trembled now, and I could see fear in his eyes, but he didn't give the box back to me. I wished Florence had cried out before I took the box out of the washer.

The man ran out of the kitchen, then through the living room toward the front door. Holding the gun in front of him, he pushed open the door and peered out.

Florence screamed again. I was certain the cry could be heard clear down in Carbon City. He was perched on the porch railing as usual.

"It's only a big bird," the man said. "Shoo! Get out of here!"

Florence stayed on the porch rail.

The man opened the door farther and raised his hand, pointing the gun at the peacock.

"No!" I cried. "Don't shoot him!" Aunt Ethel wouldn't be able to bear it if this man killed Florence. I leaped toward him, hitting his arm just as he pulled the trigger.

BAM!

I'd deflected the man's arm enough so the bullet hit one of the porch posts but missed the peacock. Florence flapped away to roost in the chestnut tree.

My racing heart throbbed in my ears. I was certain the man would turn on me next. I had saved Florence, but at what cost?

Instead of shooting me, the man ran to his car, got in, and started the engine.

I closed the door and locked it in case he changed his mind and came back.

I tried to read the license plate number through the window, but the car was beyond the light from the porch. It was so dark I couldn't even tell what color car the man drove.

As the red taillights moved down the driveway, my knees shook so much I had to lean against the window ledge. Relief that I was still alive mixed with dismay that the thief had gotten away with the money.

I had tried my best to stop him, and so had Willie, but our best had not been good enough. I slumped onto the couch and closed my eyes, fighting back tears.

•

CHAPTER NINETEEN

A shrill sound sliced through the black night, but this time it wasn't the peacock. Sirens rose and fell, close by!

I rushed to the window and saw the red taillights still in the driveway. The thief's car stood nose to nose with a police car. Blue lights whirled, sending flashes of color across the trees.

The police car had entered Aunt Ethel's driveway before the thief could drive out.

A second police car pulled in directly behind the first one. The sirens died. Two people in uniform got out of each car and approached the thief's car with their guns drawn.

I ran out to the porch. "He's armed!" I shouted. "He has a gun!"

The police officers surrounded the car. One of

them opened the driver's door. The man stepped out with his empty hands over his head. He was not wearing the ski mask.

As I cautiously approached the cars, I heard one of the officers say, "Aaron Turlep? What are you doing here?"

"I might ask the same of you," the man said. "I came to visit Ethel Hodge, but she isn't home."

The officer turned to one of the other officers. "This is Aaron Turlep," he said, "manager of the Hillside Bank."

"May I put my hands down now?" the thief asked. "Clearly, you've made a mistake here and are looking for someone else, so I'll be on my way."

"No!" I shouted as I ran toward them. "There's no mistake! This man held a gun on me and threatened to kill me."

"Why?" an officer asked.

"I was planting flowers at the cemetery when I found a buried box of money. He came and made me give it to him. I think it was stolen."

The police kept their guns drawn. One of them patted down the thief while the others searched his car.

One of the officers called out from the front seat of the car, "The kid's right. There's a box full of hundred-dollar bills! There're also a handgun and a black ski mask under the seat."

"Can you explain those?" the officer who had recognized Mr. Turlep asked.

Mr. Turlep said, "I demand to call my attorney."

Mrs. Morris drove in behind the police cars. She ran to me, her red hat askew, and hugged me. "Are you all right?" she asked.

I struggled to get out of her ample grasp. "I'm fine," I said, "thanks to you."

She and I went back to her car, where we could see what happened without being in the way. Soon a police officer questioned both of us, then set a time for us to come to the police station the next morning.

Mrs. Morris had to drive her car up to the house when a police tow truck came to take Mr. Turlep's car away. As we watched from the porch, I told Mrs. Morris that Aunt Ethel had a broken ankle and was in the hospital.

Mrs. Morris wanted me to go home with her, but I said I had animals to care for, which was true.

"Then I'm spending the night here," she said. "I can sleep in Florence's room."

"You don't have to do that. With Mr. Turlep in custody, I'm not scared to stay by myself."

"I know you aren't, but I wouldn't sleep a wink

knowing you're out here by yourself." Since Aunt Ethel's telephone wasn't working, she gave one of the police officers her daughter's phone number and asked him to let her family know where she was.

As soon as the tow truck left, the two squad cars left, also, with Mr. Turlep in the backseat of the first one.

I fed Florence, who seemed no worse for his encounter with Willie, and took a shower. Then Mrs. Morris and I finished off the chocolate chip cookies.

Although I really wasn't scared, I did lock all the doors before Mrs. Morris and I went upstairs.

Bed had never felt better, but I was too keyed up to fall asleep right away. I lay thinking about everything that had happened. I wished Willie would show up, so I could thank him for helping me. If he had not come and distracted Mr. Turlep by pushing the phone to the floor and breaking a plate and making Florence screech, I wouldn't have been able to keep Mr. Turlep there long enough. He would have gotten away with the money before the police arrived.

I wondered why Willie had come when I called. I'd already moved his leg bones, so he didn't have anything to gain by helping me. Was he keeping his end of the bargain? He had said he didn't ever go places he had not been when he was alive, yet he came when I needed help. He had used up all his strength trying to scare Mr. Turlep.

I wondered how Aunt Ethel was. I hoped she'd come home tomorrow. I had expected the summer here to be dull, but Aunt Ethel made it interesting. I'd eaten spaghetti for breakfast and pancakes for dinner; I'd met a peacock and helped a stray cat; I'd even learned to knit.

Even though I didn't agree with everything Aunt Ethel did, such as shoot the bat, I liked her.

Gradually I relaxed, and when I closed my eyes, I thought about Mom and Steven. I hoped they were all right; I hoped everything was going well for them in India. I wasn't angry at them anymore. My close brush with death had erased my resentment about spending the summer here. Baseball isn't quite as important when a gun is pointed at your heart.

Florence woke me early, as usual. I fed him, grabbed a muffin for myself, and hurried to the tree house to be sure Mrs. Stray and her kittens had food and water. The food dish was empty, so I refilled it.

I didn't see the cats or Willie, and I couldn't wait because Muriel Morris and I were going to the police station in Diamond Hill. We had to give our official accounts of what had happened and sign affidavits.

"We need to leave early enough for me to stop at home and change clothes," she said.

On our way to town, she said, "That was the best night's sleep I've had in years. It was so quiet! I never woke up once."

I waited in the car while she went into her apartment to change. She came out wearing a different purple dress and a different red hat. This one had a broad brim with a big purple bow.

"You're the talk of the town," she told me. "My phone rang three times while I was trying to get ready. The whole county is in shock over Aaron Turlep getting caught with a gun and stolen money."

She switched on the car radio; a news station was giving details of Mr. Turlep's arrest. It seemed odd to hear the radio announcer broadcast details of something I had actually experienced.

When we got to the police station, two of the officers who had arrested Mr. Turlep the night before took our statements. I explained again how I happened to find the box.

Mrs. Morris told them she couldn't believe her eyes when she saw the word *HELP* written in frosting on her daughter's birthday cake.

"I almost asked Josh if this was supposed to be a

joke," she said, "but then I saw the look in his eyes, and I knew his plea for help was real. Also, I'd seen Ethel's truck parked outside so I knew the story of her going to Carbon City wasn't true. As soon as I was out of sight of Ethel's house, I tried to use my cell phone to call for help, but I was out of range, so I drove straight to the Carbon City Market and used the phone there to call you. I didn't know what was wrong at Ethel's house, but I knew Josh needed help in a hurry. I'd seen a car I didn't recognize parked at Ethel's house, but Josh didn't answer when I asked who it belonged to."

"Josh, if you hadn't been able to stall the thief," the officer said, "we might not have made it in time. You used your head and did everything you could to keep Mr. Turlep there for as long as possible."

"I didn't want to give him the money. He said it was his, but I didn't believe him."

"You only gave it up when you had to, in order to save your own life. That was the smart thing to do."

"It's lucky we caught Turlep with the ski mask, the gun, and the money in his car," the other officer said. "If we hadn't, he would never have been a suspect. Friday was his last day at the bank. He had told everyone he was retiring and moving to Florida; he would have gone as planned. We had no reason to think he had stolen cash with him."

Mrs. Morris said, "I've known Aaron Turlep for thirty years, and I would never have suspected him. It's sad to see someone who's respected in the community throw away the rest of his life. If he needed money in his retirement, he could have worked part-time in Florida. He could have been a guide on a fishing boat or done something else he enjoyed. Instead, he stole what didn't belong to him."

The officer said, "The only fish Mr. Turlep will see in retirement are the ones served for dinner on Fridays in the state prison."

"Do you think the money is from the Cash for Critters auction?" I asked.

"It is," the officer said. "We examined it last night."

"How can you be sure?" Mrs. Morris asked. "Even though the total amount is the same, how can you prove where it came from unless you know the serial numbers of some of the stolen money?"

The police officer smiled. "We can prove it," he said, "thanks to my grandchildren."

"Your grandchildren!" I said. "How do they figure in this?"

"Back when we had the auction, Lexi and Krista earned money to help the animals. They were eight and ten years old then; they did chores for my wife and me and for their other grandparents. They even had a Cash for Critters lemonade stand. When it came time to turn in their earnings, I told them I'd match what they had raised. Since they each had earned almost fifty dollars, I took their money and gave both of them a one-hundred-dollar bill to take to the auction."

"That could still be any one-hundred-dollar bill," Mrs. Morris said.

"Let me finish the story. Before we left home to go to the auction, Lexi and Krista took a red pencil and printed *For the animals* on their money. When the money was stolen, I alerted every bank in the state to watch for those words on a one-hundred-dollar bill. The two bills never surfaced until last night. They were both in the box Josh found."

"For the animals," I said, thinking of Mrs. Stray and her kittens. "All that money is for the animals."

"We'll finally get our animal shelter," Mrs. Morris said.

"There's one thing I can't figure out," the officer said. "After we arrested him last night, Mr. Turlep kept mentioning a ghost. I've never heard stories of the old Hodge place being haunted."

"Before I gave Mr. Turlep the money," I said, "I told him there was a ghost in the room. I was trying to scare him so he would leave." As much as I liked Muriel Morris and the police officers, I didn't want to tell them the truth about Willie. He was my special secret friend, and I wanted to keep it that way.

"Mr. Turlep was superstitious," Mrs. Morris said. "I worked at the bank for a short time years ago, and I used to joke about it with one of the other employees. Mr. Turlep wouldn't step on a sidewalk crack or walk under a ladder, and he disliked Friday the thirteenth. Telling him you saw a ghost was probably the best thing you could have done to make him nervous."

The officer walked with us to the door. A reporter and cameraman waited outside.

"Is this the boy who found the money?" the reporter asked.

The police officer told me, "You don't have to talk to them if you don't want to."

"I don't mind."

The reporter stepped closer, and the camera turned toward me. Too bad Aunt Ethel didn't have a TV set so I could watch myself later.

When we were finished talking to the news crew, Mrs. Morris drove me to the hospital to visit Aunt Ethel.

"Will you come in with me?" I asked. "I have to be accompanied by an adult because I'm not sixteen yet."

"Of course I'm going in. I can't wait to tell Ethel about all the excitement."

As we walked down the hospital corridor, Mrs. Morris said, "I have a grandson your age. Maybe you'd like to go with me to one of Bruce's baseball games. I watch all of them."

"Sure!" I said. "I was supposed to be on a baseball team myself this summer, back in Minneapolis."

Before we reached Aunt Ethel's room, we heard her shouting, "Fleas and mosquitoes! This isn't what I asked for."

"Oh, oh," Mrs. Morris said. "It sounds as if Ethel is back to normal."

When we reached the doorway, we saw a nurse, hands on hips, standing beside Aunt Ethel's bed. "This is a hospital, not a restaurant," the nurse said. "I can't request breakfast items that are not on the menu."

"How can you expect the patients to get well if you don't feed us our vegetables?" Aunt Ethel demanded.

"For breakfast?" the nurse said.

Mrs. Morris entered the room. "Never mind, dear. I brought you some baby carrots from my garden and some lovely ripe strawberries from the fruit stand."

"That's better," Aunt Ethel said. "She wanted me to eat oatmeal at this time of day."

The nurse walked to the door, shaking her head. "She was demanding mashed potatoes and spinach," she said. "For breakfast!"

"I hope you're here to take me home," Aunt Ethel said.

"Will the doctor let you go?" Mrs. Morris asked.

"He will as long as someone stays with me. Josh, you're now the official nurse. All you have to do is make sure I keep my foot elevated for a few days."

"No problem."

"You couldn't be in more capable hands," Mrs. Morris said. "Have you heard the news?"

"What news?"

"You didn't see the television reports?"

"You know I don't watch television. What happened?"

"You really should watch the news," Muriel said. "If you did, you'd know what happened at your place last night. Josh is a hero!" She began a detailed account of Mr. Turlep's actions and mine.

Aunt Ethel kept shaking her head in disbelief. "I

leave you alone for one night," she said, "and all this happens!"

"The police are sure it's the money for the animal shelter," Mrs. Morris said. "They recovered all of it, one hundred thirty thousand dollars."

Aunt Ethel clapped her hands. "As soon as I can, Josh, I'll bake you a Thank You from the Animals cake."

"Chocolate, please," I said.

It took another two hours to get a prescription from the hospital pharmacy and written instructions for Aunt Ethel's care. Aunt Ethel fidgeted and complained the whole time.

Finally she told the nurse, "If you don't release me in the next ten minutes, I'm leaving anyway."

CHAPTER TWENTY

Aunt Ethel protested about getting pushed to the car in a wheelchair, consenting only when Mrs. Morris pointed out that the wheelchair would be faster than walking. I think the nursing staff was glad to see us go.

We stopped on the way home from the hospital to buy cat food and to pick up the mail. I had a letter from Mom and Steven, which I read in the car.

We're working hard. It's hot—over ninety degrees every day and not much cooler at night. It rains a lot, too, because this is monsoon season. Next week we're going to visit a Hindu temple that was built in the tenth century.

*We miss you terribly. I hope the summer
isn't as bad as you feared. Write soon.*

> *Love you lots,*
> *Mom and Steven*

When we got home, Mrs. Morris helped Aunt
Ethel get settled comfortably in her recliner with the
footrest up. "I'll stay and chat a while," she said. "In
fact, it might be a good idea for me to stay in
Florence's room for a few days if you don't mind."

"Why should I mind?" Aunt Ethel asked. "Josh is
a good dishwasher, but we'll need a cook."

"It's so quiet here at night," Mrs. Morris said. "I
think I'm ready to give up my apartment and find a
house in the country where I'd have more garden
space. Would you like some tea, Ethel?"

"I'd love some."

While Aunt Ethel and Mrs. Morris drank their tea,
I went to the tree house to check on Mrs. Stray and
her kittens.

I also hoped to see Willie, so I could thank him
for helping me. I wondered what had happened when
Florence saw him. Had the peacock screamed last
night because it recognized Willie or because it was
hungry?

I sat on the ground near the cat food and waited.

I thought about my letter from Mom and Steven. I hadn't mailed any of my letters to them; they would be plenty worried if they didn't hear from me soon.

Mrs. Stray crept out of the bushes toward the food. "You'd better bring your babies out here and let me tame them," I told her. "You don't want them growing up wild in the woods."

To my surprise, Mrs. Stray let me touch her while she ate. As soon as I started to stroke her fur, a deep, rumbling purr came from her throat. I slid my hand down her back, over and over.

When she finished eating, she walked back and forth against my knee, still purring. She must have been someone's pet at one time. Had she been dumped here because her person didn't want kittens? I couldn't imagine anyone being so uncaring, yet Aunt Ethel said it happens frequently here in the country.

I saw the kittens watching from a distance. I hoped if they saw me petting their mother, they might come close, too, but they didn't.

"I have all summer," I told them. "You'll get used to me, especially when you aren't nursing anymore and I'm your only food source."

I had told Mrs. Morris about the cats. "If you can't pick them up and pet them within a day or two, we'll rent a humane trap," she said. "You can take them to my place and keep them in the spare bedroom. You and Bruce can play with them there. Kittens need to be socialized as early as possible."

Mrs. Stray drank some water, then returned to her brood.

I climbed up the ladder to the tree house. As I opened the door, I called, "Willie? Are you here?"

"I'm here. I came to say good-bye."

His voice came from outside.

I rushed to a window and opened it. I could barely make him out against the trees. Always before, he had seemed solid; now he was as transparent as a wisp of smoke.

"Good-bye?" I said. "Where are you going?"

"I'm moving on."

"No kidding! After all these years? What happened?"

"I have love in my heart." I had to lean toward him to hear the faint words. "For you. My friend."

I swallowed hard. I looked at the bearded miner with his one pant leg pinned above his knee, and I knew I loved him, too.

As I watched, the image of Willie faded away.

"Thank you for helping me last night," I called, but there was no answer. He was gone.

I knew I would never see Willie again. He was no longer a ghost; he was an angel.

I was glad for Willie but sorry for me. I would miss him.

I turned away from the window, then saw Willie's hat on the tree-house floor beside my box of books. He had taken it off before he went on and left it for me.

When I put the miner's hat on my head, I smelled coal dust. I closed my eyes, honored that my friend had left me his most prized possession. I knew I would cherish this hat, and the memory of Willie, forever.

I went back to the house to fix lunch, but Mrs. Morris had already made sandwiches. I held Aunt Ethel's arm while she walked to the table, then helped her get comfortable in her chair, with her foot propped up.

With Willie gone, I would never find out why Florence had screamed when Mr. Turlep had the gun pointed at me. Had he recognized Willie? I decided it didn't matter. Aunt Ethel was happy believing the peacock was Florence, and the peacock was happy living here; I'd leave it at that.

Mrs. Morris left after lunch to deliver her daughter's cake and birthday gift and to pack her clothes so she could stay with us a while. The telephone repairman came that afternoon, and so did two women from Aunt Ethel's church. The women brought a bouquet of snapdragons and a big bowl of potato salad. The repairman had barely left when the phone rang.

"It's Muriel," the caller said when I answered. "Bruce says his team still needs an outfielder. Would you be willing to join the team?"

Does the sun rise in the east?

"Where do they play?" I asked. "Aunt Ethel can't drive with a cast on her foot, but I could ride my bike to the games if it isn't too far."

"Oh, don't worry about getting there. Even after I move back home, I'll drive you. They play in Diamond Hill, but I always take Bruce, and you aren't far out of the way."

"That would be great," I said, even though I knew it really was out of her way. "Thanks a lot!"

"The next game is Tuesday night at seven. You'll have to go early to get a uniform."

"What about Aunt Ethel? She shouldn't stay by herself while we're both at a ball game."

"Leave that to me."

While Aunt Ethel chatted with the church ladies, I went to my room, tore up the three letters I had written, and started over.

June 20

Dear Mom and Steven,

Sorry I didn't write sooner, but I've been really busy. I'll tell you the best news first: I'm going to play on a baseball team! Aunt Ethel's friend has a grandson my age and his team needs another outfielder. Hooray!

I spend a lot of time in the tree house, and I'm feeding a stray cat and her kittens. Could I keep the cat? Please? She's already tame and could fly home in a carrier. I named her Mrs. Stray.

Aunt Ethel bakes the best cakes in the world. Her secret ingredient is sour cream. She fell and broke her ankle, so it's a good thing I'm here to help while she's in a cast. Her friend is staying here a few days, too.

Your hopeful (about the cat) son,

Josh

I decided to wait until I was home to tell about Mr. Turlep and the box of money. Mom would freak out over a thief threatening to kill me; it would be better to tell her when I was standing beside her, safe and sound. I didn't plan to tell her, or anyone, about

Willie. I was glad I'd never mailed the letter about him. The ghost and his grave would remain my secret.

Aunt Ethel's friends agreed to mail my letter on their way home. I wanted it to go out right away.

When Mrs. Morris returned, she brought a casserole and a schedule of people who had agreed to stay with Aunt Ethel while I went to my baseball games. "Now that I'm back," she told me, "you can go feed those cats."

"Cats?" Aunt Ethel said. "Plural?"

"Mrs. Stray has three kittens," I said.

"Fleas and mosquitoes! What are you going to do with four cats?"

"Bruce and I will help tame them and find homes for them," Mrs. Morris said. "I'll need a project, since I expect to stay here as long as you have that cast."

"You don't have to babysit me," Aunt Ethel said.

"I'm not," Mrs. Morris replied. "I'm here to listen to the birds. All except Florence."

I returned to the cemetery. I removed Willie's small marker, carried it uphill to the riverbank, and put it where it belonged. I wore my miner's hat the whole time.

After I put the marker securely in its place, I stepped back and looked at it.

Of course, the marker still said only W.M.M., but

in my heart it said WILBER MICHAEL MARTIN, LOVING HUSBAND, FATHER, AND FRIEND.

Especially *friend*.

Three days later, Bruce and I caught all the cats. By then I was able to pick up Mrs. Stray so it was easy to put her in one of the three cat carriers that Mrs. Morris had borrowed. After that, all it took was patience.

Bruce and I sat on the ground under the tree house, still and quiet. Beside each of us was a cat carrier with an end flap that opened down, like the ramp of a horse trailer. A small dish of tuna cat food was at the far back of each carrier.

I'd put out that kind of food for two days and had seen the kittens eat it, so I knew they would be attracted by the smell. It took almost two hours before the orange kitten timidly approached. It kept looking around as if wondering where its mother was, and it was clearly nervous about Bruce and me, but the tuna smell was more than it could resist. It walked into the carrier beside Bruce and began to eat. He quickly closed the flap, then took the carrier into the tree house, where Mrs. Stray waited in her carrier. He put the kitten in with its mother.

While he was doing that, the black-and-white kitten emerged from the woods. This one was bolder, maybe because there was only one person to watch instead of two. I held my breath, hoping Bruce wouldn't come down the ladder and scare the kitten off. The kitten kept watching me, but it marched into the carrier without hesitation.

I heard the third kitten, the one who looked like Mrs. Stray, mewing in the underbrush so I quickly climbed the ladder and put my carrier on the floor beside the one that now contained Mrs. Stray and the orange kitten.

Bruce took his empty carrier down and waited for the third kitten. This one acted the most apprehensive, so I stayed in the tree house, watching from the window. For a while, I was afraid that third kitten was never going to overcome its fear, but it finally crept forward, almost sliding on its stomach, and entered the carrier.

Bruce closed the flap. We had all of them!

Mrs. Morris had talked Aunt Ethel into letting us use her extra bedroom as the cat room. It was a perfect space. There wasn't a bed in it, and we had already pushed all the storage boxes against the wall to eliminate places for the kittens to hide. The room was ready, with fresh water, food, catnip toys, a pile of old towels for the cats to sleep on, and a litter box.

We turned the four cats loose in their new living quarters and watched them explore. From then on, I spent several hours each day playing with the kittens. Bruce came almost every day, too.

Before long the kittens let us pick them up, and soon they began purring when we held them. We named the orange one Max, the black-and-white one Purrball, and the tabby-striped one Spooky.

July 18
Dear Mom and Steven,

I can hardly believe I've already been here more than a month. I've been so busy that I haven't even read most of the books I brought with me. Instead, I've read a lot of history about the coal mines around here. Yesterday Bruce and I went to see the old coke ovens. They're like big beehives that you can walk right into.

Thanks for the box of birthday presents. The best one of all was the coupon good for me to keep Mrs. Stray. You'll really like her; she's a great cat.

Aunt Ethel made a chocolate birthday cake for me, and Bruce came for a sleepover in the tree house. That's where I was when you called to wish me happy birthday. We had a blast!

Aunt Ethel gets the cast off her foot next week. Here's the big news: Mrs. Morris is going to move in here permanently. From now on, she will do all the driving, so Aunt Ethel sold her truck. Mrs. Morris will deliver cakes so Aunt Ethel can take customers who can't pick up the cakes, and after I go home, Mrs. Morris says she'll wash the dishes.

Aunt Ethel has been coming to my baseball games. She and Mrs. Morris sit in lawn chairs and cheer for me and Bruce. Tuesday night I hit two singles and scored the winning run. Our coach took the whole team out for ice cream to celebrate. We have eight wins and three losses since I joined the team.

Max and Purrball got adopted together. One of Aunt Ethel's church friends took both of them. Bruce is keeping Spooky, and Mrs. Stray is coming home with me. Hooray!

I miss you guys, but I'm having a great summer.

Your happy teenager,
Josh